GLA
OUR HUMANITY

GW00854597

ALI KASHANIAN

outskirts press

Glances at Our Humanity
All Rights Reserved.
Copyright © 2019 Ali Kashanian
v3.0

The opinions expressed in this manuscript are solely the opinions of the author and do not represent the opinions or thoughts of the publisher. The author has represented and warranted full ownership and/or legal right to publish all the materials in this book.

This book may not be reproduced, transmitted, or stored in whole or in part by any means, including graphic, electronic, or mechanical without the express written consent of the publisher except in the case of brief quotations embodied in critical articles and reviews.

Outskirts Press, Inc.
http://www.outskirtspress.com

ISBN: 978-1-9772-0381-6

Cover Photo © 2019 www.gettyimages.com. All rights reserved - used with permission.

Outskirts Press and the "OP" logo are trademarks belonging to Outskirts Press, Inc.

PRINTED IN THE UNITED STATES OF AMERICA

Table of Contents

Acknowledgment

I LEARNED MY values from my late father. I love you, Baba Joon. I always did. I always will.

I learned to think in America. I had the best teachers at the University of New Orleans. They were the best educators, and most dedicated; they helped me develop intellectually. Thank you so much! Thank you, Uncle Sam!

Finally, I am forever grateful to so many Americans who adopted me as their countryman. Over the years I have met so many kind and generous citizens. They all made me feel at home and always made me feel welcome at their table. Thank you so much!

All stories in this book, with the exception of the one about my dear, late grandmother, are fictional. No name or event is related to anyone I have known, or met. Should it seem that way, it is completely accidental.

A VISIT TO A MOTORCYCLE DEALERSHIP

TWO YEARS APART, Samantha and Susan were the daughters of Mr. and Mrs. Forkroad. Their only brother had died in a car accident. Susan could not keep the same boyfriend for the first three years of college.

"I thought you were dating Scott. Who is Bill?"

"Scott's parents did not like me, Mom."

"What was wrong with Bill? We only met him once!"

"I didn't like his friends, and he talked too much, Dad."

"What was wrong with Jacob?"

"He's a college dropout, Sam! I won't date a loser."

Susan always had a convenient excuse for breaking up with her boyfriends.

"You're only good at losing boyfriends," Samantha always told her, as their mother sighed.

Several months before her graduation, Susan brought home a new guy. A few years older and very polite, he was very different than her previous boyfriends. He finished his sentences and had perfect diction.

"I like David. He is going to law school! Are you going to keep him?" Susan's father asked.

"I will, if he graduates at the top of his class, as he has promised me," Susan responded.

"I might be good at losing boyfriends, but I am also good at finding a good husband," Susan told Samantha with sarcasm. Susan received her college degree, and David finished law school. He found a lucrative job in Lake Charles, and she found a job in a local company. "We're going to get married. I'll find another job," Susan told her parents.

Susan's parents did not want their daughter to live in another city, but they were gaining a son-in-law and their daughter was happy. They really liked David. He was an overachiever, reliable, kind, and caring; and he adored their daughter.

The two mothers were surprised to learn that neither Susan, nor David, wanted to have a big wedding. They had found a house in Lake Charles. David's father was giving them a lump sum of cash, as a wedding present. He was also helping them to finance the house. Susan had asked her father to help them with the down payment, as a wedding present.

"We have some savings of our own, Dad, but it is not very much."

Samantha and her high school sweetheart, John, were also planning to get married, but she insisted on a big wedding.

"Mom, Dad, I'll only marry once."

They were going to move in with John's parents after the wedding. Both working full-time, they were planning to save their money and buy their own house. John wanted to stay with the same company and become an assistant manager.

"Hi, Penny! I like your shoes," Susan said.

Penny smiled bashfully.

"Where's your brother?" Susan asked.

"He's with Grandma and Grandpa, Aunt Susan."

"When are you coming to Lake Charles? We bought a new house with a big yard. It has a swimming pool too!"

"Dad always works and Mom is always with my baby brother, Aunt Susan." Like any child at her age, she could not hide her sadness and disappointment.

"Sweetheart, your father is an assistant manager now. He has a lot of responsibility. Come here and sit on my lap. Tell me about Hammond. Uncle David and I have never been there."

"I don't like Hammond! I don't see Grandma and Grandpa anymore!"

For a brief moment Susan reconsidered

her plans to become a mother.

"Pumpkin, I want to talk to Aunt Susan and Uncle David. Would you find Daddy and tell him we are here. Grandma and Grandpa were asking about you too."

As Penny was leaving them, Samantha smiled and whispered, "She's a handful."

Susan nodded and returned a smile.

"Tell me about your new house. And you, David! You have your own law firm now!"

David smiled and said, "I'm just a partner."

"Senior partner!" Susan corrected him. Her voice conveyed pride and arrogance.

"You tell me about yourself first," she said. "You bought a bigger house in Hammond, and John is an assistant manager now!"

"He's making a little bit more money now, but he's always working." Samantha sighed. "God knows we need every penny of what he makes, and I have to stay home with the kids all the time. We should've gone to college, like you guys. I should've made him go to college."

"Isn't he going to college now?" David asked.

"He's doing it part-time, and his dad is paying the tuition. But please don't mention it to Mom and Dad. Don't embarrass him!"

"Do you guys need money?" Susan and David asked simultaneously.

"Oh no! You'll embarrass him even more."

This was the wedding of their cousin, and it was held at the atrium of a big hotel. David and Susan were staying in the hotel. Samantha and John were planning to drive home after the wedding. That was before John and David discovered a new cocktail. They were drinking like two young college students.

"Why don't you stay at the hotel with us tonight? We have a suite for the entire weekend," David said.

"But we were planning to drive home," John said, making a meek objection.

Susan's father overheard the conversation. "Don't be stubborn, John. You're in no condition to drive back to Hammond. If you don't want to stay in the hotel, we can all go home in our SUV."

"We're taking the grandchildren with us home anyway," said Mrs. Forkroad.

It was eleven the next morning. "Mom, Dad, we bought some donuts," Susan said, as they put two dozen donuts on the kitchen counter.

"How is David doing? Does he have a big hangover?" Mrs. Forkroad whispered to Susan.

"He's doing fine, Mom," Susan said, chuckling. "He went jogging this morning. 'That's the best cure for hangover,' he said." Susan was not exactly whispering.

Mrs. Forkroad shook her head. "John did the same thing. I wouldn't believe it, had I not seen it with my own eyes."

"They are crazy, Mom. You have two crazy guys as your sons-in-law."

"Don't you talk that way about my sons," said Mr. Forkroad.

"He's my husband, Dad!"

"And he's my son-in-law."

"I know, Dad. According to you David can do no wrong. He's just an angel."

"What are you guys going to do? It's a nice day," said Mrs. Forkroad.

"I don't know. I'm sure David and John will come up with a good plan. Sam told me he had two days off. Me, I just want to help David spend his money."

"Why don't you leave the grandchildren with us? You guys are still young. Go out there and have some fun."

Thirty minutes later David and John were talking about motorcycles. "Dad, we're going to look at Harley-Davidson motorcycles. We're going to buy one. Why don't you and Mom join us?"

"We have plans of our own," said Mr. Forkroad, looking at Penny and grinning.

"Ice cream, Grandpa?" Penny was smiling and showing her teeth.

"Ice cream and movies." Mr. Forkroad looked happier than his granddaughter.

This was the very first time for Samantha and Susan to visit a Harley-Davidson dealership. Bikers, male and female, wore leather vests with peculiar patches of different sizes.

Some of them looked like the characters at prison yards, shown on TV. Their thick arms, entirely covered with tattoos, were completely exposed. Some had long untended beards and mustaches.

"Are you thinking what I'm thinking?" Susan asked her sister in a whisper.

"Shut up. You'll get us in trouble," Samantha whispered back.

They were glad that the kids had stayed with the grandparents. David noticed it immediately and led Samantha and Susan to a different section of the store, where they sold T-shirts, jackets, helmets, boots, and sundry biker goods. This was a different world. The entire family, moms and dads—with their children—all dressed like normal shoppers in a mall, were walking casually and sifting through everything.

"Honey, I want you to pick a T-shirt for everybody. You have to get one for Mom and one for Dad," David said.

"Aren't you forgetting your parents?"

"Them too! Everybody! You and Sam have to pick them. John and I will be looking at motorcycles."

"I'm sure you will. As long as you're not buying anything," Susan said and gave him one of her clear and well-understood—don't-even-think-about-it—looks.

"Dad gave me one of his credit cards. He made me promise to spend a hundred dollars on the kids," Samantha told John.

"Honey!" John protested. "Why did you take his credit card? He's taking our kids to the movies. Knowing my daughter, she'll make him buy them everything at the mall."

"You know my father. He won't take no for an answer. They are his grandchildren. I'll just buy them two small gifts to make him happy."

Several young ladies were working there who reminded Susan of her college days. "This must be your first time here," said one of them. She had a pleasant smile and a caring voice. "We have a big selection of T-shirts," she added, after introducing herself.

"We really don't have that much money to spend. The boys have the money," Susan said.

"Pick up everything you like. "I'll make the boys pay for all of them," an older female employee said, chuckling. She was the manager and she seemed just as pleasant.

Samantha looked at the young female employee and said sheepishly, "I just have to buy two small presents for my kids to make my father happy. My son is two and my daughter is four years old." After a moment of hesitation, she added timidly, "I have my father's credit card. Is it okay to use it?"

"Of course! We don't really like money here. We prefer credit cards."

Of all the noises, one was very clear to John and David and it came from different directions. "Uncle Chuck."

"Uncle Chuck."

"Wha's up?" "Wha's up?" responded a man with a big grin.

"Uncle Chuck. What's up?"

"Uncle Chuck. What's up?"

Who is Uncle Chuck? they asked themselves.

It did not take but a few minutes before an older salesman by the name of Bob, approached John and David. They made the mistake of telling Bob they did not ride a motorcycle. "Why not?" Bob asked with a comely smile. His question was direct, but they did not feel pressured by him.

Bob told them he had two cousins in Lake Charles and two in Hammond. "I know the fire marshal in Hammond," he told them and kept mentioning names and places in both cities. "You're an attorney and I know the chief of police in Lake Charles. I know him personally." With laughter he added, "I guess I won't have to worry about speeding in your city anymore."

"Bob, line one! Coach, line one!" was announced through the intercom. "Bob, line one. Coach, line one!" "Coach, customer is here to see you at the showroom," was said through another loud speaker.

"That guy knew a lot about motorcycles," said John, after Bob excused himself and walked toward the front of store. He was greeting longtime customers throughout the store, and everybody called him Coach. "Do you think he knew all those people?" John asked David.

David smiled. Without uttering a word he had answered John.

"Hi, I'm Jack, the sales manager," Jack told John and David, as soon as Bob walked away.

Born in Texas, Jack had lived there for many years, including his college years. He did not know anyone in Hammond, but he claimed to have three cousins in Lake Charles.

"I know the chief of police in Lake Charles. As a matter of fact we took courses in college together," Jack told David.

"Well, it's good to know," David said. "I always thought the chief went to LSU," he added with a smirk.

Jack did not flinch and responded quickly. "He did. Absolutely! I had one summer semester at LSU. We took a course in Southern Christianity together." With straight a face, he added, "That was when I met the chief."

"Wha's up? Wha's up? You must be noo," said a middle-aged man with a friendly demeanor. They shook hands and he introduced himself to John and David as Uncle Chuck. Uncle Chuck was wearing a leather vest with many patches. He had a benevolent smile and a friendly demeanor. They understood very little of what he said, other than "CVO" and "Kaz."

John and David were politely listening and nodding as Samantha and Susan approached them. "We have picked ten T-shirts and two jackets for the kids. You guys have to see them."

"Honey, this is Uncle Chuck. Did you know we can renew our wedding vows on a motorcycle today," David told Susan enthusiastically.

"Talk to Kaz. Kaz is the man. He tek ker of you," said Uncle Chuck.

An hour later, John and David were sitting with Kaz and Cliff, at two different tables. "Kaz is a really nice guy, but we could not understand everything he said," David told Cliff.

Cliff smiled. "Kaz is something else. Sometimes we don't understand him either, but he is honest and trustworthy."

"Oh, I have no doubt about it. Everybody here had good things to say about him, but I'm not buying a bike today. You have to persuade my wife, and she won't go for it."

"Absolutely! We understand. Didn't Kaz explain it to you? You're just taking some numbers to go home and have a kitchen table talk with your wife."

"Honey, this is a CVO Street Glide. Bret rides one *just like this!"* David told Susan.

"Kaz told me it is forty-two thousand dollars!"

"That sounds right." David was not going to tell Susan, but his partner, Bret, had spent fifty thousand dollars for his bike. And that was a good deal, the partners thought.

"Why is this one so expensive? The one Kaz was showing John was sixteen!"

"Honey, John was looking at a used Heritage. This is a 117 CVO Street Glide."

"But John's dirt bike was a 250. This one is only 117?"

"Didn't you hear Kaz explaining it to us? This is 117 cubic inch. That would be equal to 1,900 CC. John's dirt bike was only 250 CC."

"Ma'am, this is the Cadillac of all Harleys. Just look at it! We have a hundred bikes in this showroom, and this one stands out. It's in a class by itself, ma'am," Cliff explained.

"We explained to Kaz. We're not buying anything today," Susan told Cliff.

"I understand. You just want to renew your wedding vows. Kaz explained everything to me."

"Kaz to the sales tower! Kaz to the sales

tower!" announced, Ken, the store manager. Kaz and Cliff had submitted two individual credit apps for John and David.

"There is something you have to know. John and David___"

Ken did let Kaz finish his sentence. "Kaz! Kaz! They don't have an endorsement. How am I supposed to let them test drive?"

"They just want to renew their vows. You see, David and Susan did not have a wedding. John____"

"Kaz! Kaz!" Jack interjected this time. "You're killing me! You're not a social worker anymore. You're not a patient advocate. You're selling a___"

This time Kaz interjected. "Uncle Chuck is going to let David and Susan renew their vows on his bike, and Mad Dog is willing to let John and Sam renew their vows on his bike."

"Who is Mad Dog?" asked Scott, the general manager.

"He is the one who is talking with John and his wife, right now!" Kaz said and pointed at them with his head.

"That guy? You know him?" Jack asked,

and momentarily became reticent. "I love you, Kaz, but that guy!? He is a gorilla! Just look at his arms! He'll break every bone in your body, if his bike is scratched."

"Mad Dog wants to give me one of his guns! Do you know how many times he has asked me to ride his bike?"

"It's scary, but I don't think Kaz is making it up, guys. He doesn't lie!" Cliff said. He was shaking his head, as if this scenario would have been unimaginable for anyone other than Kaz.

Ken was looking at the bank response as everybody else was picking on Kaz. He turned to the general manager. "Wow! Look at this, Scotty. Harley has approved him for a fifty-thousand-dollar loan. *With no down payment*!"

"Good job, guys. Good job, Kaz," Scott said. "Let me see what we have on John." He looked at his computer screen. "It looks like John has been approved for a loan too. By Harley. He does not need a down payment. Let's get these guys to the booth, Ken. Cliff, Kaz, keep your eyes on them."

Susan and Samantha were surprised to learn that both Uncle Chuck and Mad Dog were insisting that John and David ride their bikes to the tent for the renewal of their wedding vows.

"Are you sure about this, Uncle Chuck?" Susan asked several times.

Samantha could not call Mad Dog by his nickname. "Are you sure, James? Your bike is so nice! It looks so expensive! I'm afraid, John might scratch it."

Mad Dog smiled proudly. "I take care of my bike, but I want you and John to join the Harley family. Don't worry about it. He won't scratch it."

Everyone was in the parking lot for the ceremony. Susan had tears in her eyes, as she was renewing her vows. The husband and wife could not keep their eyes off each other. This was the moment they had been looking forward to for so many years. Susan looked at everybody as she wiped her tears of joy. She finally had her wedding, and no motorcycle ride could have brought her more pleasure.

"Thank you so much, Scott!" Susan could

not stop thanking everybody. "You guys are the best ever," she told Kaz and Cliff. "What do you think?" she asked, whispering in David's ear.

"I can ride Bret's bike any time I want. Why should I spend fifty thousand dollars," David whispered back.

John and Samantha really wanted to buy the bike. Kaz and Cliff assured them that the bike would be delivered to their house, in Hammond.

"I have a trailer, John," Mad Dog said. "If Scotty doesn't do it for free, I will put it on my trailer and bring it to your house. We can do it together, brother."

Samantha wanted the bike more than her husband, but guilt was eating her up. Several hours earlier, she was really scared to look at Mad Dog, but now he was like a member of the family, except the fact that she could not look into his eyes without feeling ashamed.

"You know we can't let you do that, James. It doesn't feel right to put you through so much trouble. You have done so much for us. We just have to come back for the bike."

"You promise, Sam. My brother here really wants the bike. I know you want it too."

"We'll buy it. Just not today," Samantha told Mad Dog. She was very sincere.

A STORMY NIGHT IN PINEVILLE

This story is dedicated to Agnes.

IT HAPPENED IN Pineville, Louisiana, on one stormy night. Depending on who is reading this story, it could be small and insignificant, or most beautiful and unforgettable.

The Deep South has been known for romance and gentility. But we are not talking about New Orleans; we are talking about Pineville.

This was an ordinary neighborhood with

no wealthy neighbors, but every house had a sizeable front yard. All front yards were carpeted with Saint Augustine grass, and some home owners had added their own personal touch to it. One had a small flowerbed right in front of the building. A few others had evergreen shrubs, pruned hedges and holly.

The house on 621 Mathew Street was the modest one in the neighborhood. Its occupants, Jason and Angel, a happily married couple, never compared their house with any others. They had only one big oak tree in their front yard, and "majestic" was the word that popped into their head, every time they looked at the old tree. They had put a new roof on their house and bought a two-year-old Nissan Versa about three years ago. The total cost of the roof and a sizeable down payment for the car was saved by the husband and wife over several years. At that time the wife had considered repainting the front of the house, but her husband talked her out of it.

"Honey, we don't have any money set aside for painting the house. The house is all ours. You don't really want to borrow any money against the house. Do you!?"

Jason and Angel had not accumulated a lot. Their furniture was old and neither one wished to own anything for the sake of owning it or showing it off. They had no debt aside from twelve more small monthly notes on their car.

It was getting dark when Jason stepped out of his car in the driveway. He paused and looked at the paint. The orange paint had faded quite a bit. Every time he came home late from work he felt guilty about not repainting the house. He could have found a way to do it, but he hated the color orange, Angel's favorite color, and he knew she would not have agreed to any other color. He sighed and whispered to himself, "Angel knows how much I love her. She forgives me."

Sitting on their old sofa in the living room and reading another novel, Angel closed the paperback and turned around as soon as Jason entered the house. She saw him straight through the open space above the kitchen sink.

"They made you work late again?"

He walked into the living room and kissed her gently. "I meant to call you, but it was crazy at work and I didn't have a chance. Did you eat dinner?"

Angel smiled at Jason instead of answering his question. She had eaten earlier and felt guilty about it.

"I made you some pork chops. Are you hungry?" she asked.

He collapsed on the big chair on the side of their sofa and looked at her with a winsome smile. "Would you like to eat with me?"

"You look tired. I'll make you a plate," she said and set a TV tray right in front of him.

Nothing gave Angel more pleasure than fixing a plate for her husband. She would do it in a heartbeat, even if she was exhausted.

Jason did not like anyone to fix him a plate, or anything else he could do himself, and her willingness troubled him even more. "Honey, you're my wife, not my maid," he used to tell her in the early years of their marriage.

"Make yourself a plate too. Please have dinner with me?" Jason said. He moved the TV tray a few inches forward, pressed his hands on the sides of the armchair and attempted to stand up and walk to the kitchen. The chair squeaked and he sat back.

"You had a big day at work. I'll make us two plates," she said, walking to the kitchen. *I should've waited for him. He would've waited for me,* she thought.

Sprawling on the chair and surfing channels, Jason craned his neck and asked "What do you want to watch?"

"Whatever you like," she replied with no hesitation. She was patiently fixing him a plate.

He *was* hungry. Very hungry. But he was at home and nothing else mattered. *I won't starve. Take your time,* he thought, and continued looking at her. He regretted some of the things they had done years ago. *Those old days. We used to fuss at each other over nothing. Why was I so ugly about her making me a plate of dinner? Why did we nag so much?*

"Is this enough?" she asked, handing him a full plate. There were two pork chops, and generous portions of smothered potatoes and green peas on the plate.

"I'm starving and this smells really good, but what about you?"

"Weren't you watching me? My plate is in the kitchen." She paused and resisted saying, Stop worrying about me. "You start eating. I'll be right back with my plate."

She came back within seconds and he was gulping down his food. She grabbed a second TV tray, set it up, and started eating slowly.

"I love pork chops! This is really good!" he said with a mouthful.

"*I know!* Pork chops *are* your favorite. Enjoy your food." She could not keep her eyes off him. "There're plenty more in the kitchen. Let me know if you want a second plate."

"I'm the only one who eats food around here," he said with a smile that suppressed guilt.

"You always say that, honey. I eat!"

"You just eat snacks. *I* eat the food in this house."

"Why do you always do this to yourself? Stop feeling so guilty! Enjoy your food!" She sighed. "You work very hard and pay for everything! You're a good provider!"

Jason always felt that he was receiving more—far more—than he was giving in their relationship. Angel always thought he was wrong and she had told him many times.

Some fifteen minutes later, Jason's plate was empty and Angel had not touched her pork chop. "I can't eat anymore. Why don't you finish my plate?"

"You can't just live on potatoes and green peas," Jason protested mildly.

"You know me. I take small bites here and there. I don't have your appetite."

Jason wanted to insist, but his wife was a finicky eater and she never ate a complete meal.

He started eating her pork chop. "You're giving me that look again. That smile."

"I just like to see you eating. I know you don't have a chance to eat at work."

"No. You look at me as though I have made the world your oyster."

"You have. You know you have. You've given me everything I want."

Jason sighed and shook his head. *Just look around you. What have I given you, aside from a half-empty refrigerator? You could've done a lot better. A lot better than me.*

"I've cooked three more pork chops. I want you to take them to work tomorrow."

"What about you?"

"I *knew* you were going to say that! Take two of them, if you're going to feel guilty about it. I promise to eat the last one for lunch." Smiling, she added, "That way, your poor wife won't starve to death."

"I'll take two pork chops to work, if you'll walk with me in the neighborhood."

She shrugged. "Really? You'd make me walk with you at this time of the night?"

"Honey! It's not me. Your doctor wants you to be active. I'm not asking you to ride my bike. I'm not asking you to exercise. We just walk one block in the neighborhood."

"I know. You just want me to be healthy. Like you!"

She leaned on him as they walked. "You're a good man. I'm so lucky to have you."

"You're giving me too much credit. Thank you for walking with me."

That night, like every other night, the

husband and wife held each other in the bed and talked about everything. She was getting sleepy and he was tossing and turning.

"I don't want to keep you up all night. At least one of us has to sleep," Jason whispered to Angel and got out of the bed around midnight.

Jason had insomnia. He spent some of the wee hours reading, or watching TV, every night.

"Did you get enough sleep last night?" Angel asked Jason, as he was kissing her goodbye in the morning.

"I slept enough. How about you?"

"I sleep like a baby, every night. It's you I'm concerned about."

"I'll be fine, honey. Go back to sleep."

It was years ago, when Jason met Angel. At the time, they were much younger and had finally found their dream jobs. They could finally apply their education as it was meant to be, but neither one was making the merited income. Jason reminisced about his college years, an extended youthfulness. He was still very active physically, and aging had not diminished this, at least not noticeably. Until recently, Jason preferred riding a bicycle, as he did in his college years, rather than driving a car. Neither Angel nor her siblings could quite understand Jason's eccentric behavior, but they accepted him because of his other qualities.

These days they were both over sixty years old. She had several medical issues, could not work anymore, and had to see her doctors regularly to maintain her health. The two of them kept good records of her doctors' appointments and always drove to the doctor's office together. She rarely left the house without him, and occasionally giggled, "We'll have another date," referring to a doctor's visit.

He wanted to take her to the mall, or an inexpensive restaurant, once in a while. But very rare and extremely quick window shopping was all she would do.

Angel always complained about Jason's refusal to see a doctor. "You're not young anymore. You have to see a doctor," she nagged regularly for six months when Jason hurt his right knee. He had occasional and severe pain and limped all the time.

"It'll go away," he repeated until it did go away and he could walk normally and ride his bicycle again. Jason had the annoying habit of ignoring genuine medical problems. He always had the same response to Angel's concern. "It'll go away. It always will." Somehow, as Jason had predicted, his problems always went away. But he had to put up with a lot of pain and inconvenience, and that was too much for Angel to bear.

Jason hid nothing from Angel, other than putting money aside for rainy days every now and again. Angel knew it and was never bothered by it. They always spent the money together—on *their* rainy days.

"What do you have there?" one of the employees asked Jason, as they were sitting in the employees' lunch room.

"Pork chops. My Angel cooked them for me yesterday."

"Oh, yeah! It smells really good. I bet it tastes good too. You have to ask her cook for you every day! Your old lady knows how to cook."

"She's a good woman. She would do anything for me."

"Go home, Jason. Spend some quality time with your wife," the store manager said, patting Jason's shoulder.

Jason paused and looked at him with a wide-open mouth. "It's not even five o'clock," he said.

"I don't believe it! I'm trying to send you home early. And you're arguing with me? Why do you care? You're not on hourly wages." Jason stopped working, but hesitated to get up. "Go home, Jason. If you like, I'll make you work twice as hard tomorrow."

"You're home early. What happened?"

"I didn't work nearly as hard today."

"I can see. You don't look tired. Are you hungry?"

Standing in the kitchen, they stared at each other. For a moment, it was as if they were the only two occupants of the planet Earth. He held her face, and said, "I love you very much." They hugged and neither one of them wanted to let go.

Angel could not believe it. On this particular night, Jason, the man with thinning gray hair, the man who ate as if he was an eighteen-year-old football player, had no appetite. He just wanted to hold his wife. She tried very hard to remember the last time Jason had acted this way. Jason was caring and romantic, she always thought. *But this?*

As they were snuggling in front of the TV and eating popcorn, Jason said, "Let me guess. You had shredded wheat and milk for breakfast, and two slices of bread and a slice of bologna for lunch." He poked her gently and asked, "How am I doing so far?"

Holding him tighter, Angel nodded,

smiled, and drawled, "And the pork chops, as you had commanded me."

"Not plural," he said, smiling. "There was only one left."

"And I ate it, as you wished, my king." She paused. "Are you ready for dinner now?"

"Not quite yet. I kind of like what we're doing."

She put her head on his shoulder. Momentarily, she envied him for having insomnia. *I wish I could stay up all night. We could hold each other all night.*

"Are you planning to sleep at the store tonight?" the store manager asked Jason.

"I'm not done yet."

"You're done for the day. Go home, Jason!"

"Drive carefully. It'll be stormy out there," another manager said and patted Jason's shoulder.

Jason noticed some dark clouds in the sky, but it was not raining.

Driving home, Jason was thinking about

Angel. Too often, she had been standing in the kitchen, behind the main entrance door, waiting for him. He knew that was her way. She cared too much for him and worried about him. Still, this was unsettling for Jason. Jason had suspected that the noises from their driveway had brought her to the door on those occasions.

After parking their car, he stared at the car key and hesitated to push the lock button. *I shouldn't do it. It'll make too much noise*. Instead, he put the key in his pocket. He thought about locking his car in the old-fashioned way, but he was eager to go inside. *I'll come back later and lock it up. It'll be fine. No one will mess with our car here*. Standing at the door to their house, he put his key in the lock and looked at the sky again. The clouds had become dark and ominous. He stood there, just thinking. Jason had very little regret about his life. He worked very hard, but that was just his way. He liked the people at work and they liked him. Still, he relished thinking about little things that were important to him, things that were unnoticed and insignificant to many of his associates. *I don't think Angel will go for a walk tonight. Who would blame her?* More often than not, Angel put up a fight when he asked her to walk in the neighborhood with him. It was a good fight. He did not really feel like imposing his will on her. The walk, their moments together, were endearing and very special for both of them. They enjoyed holding hands and Jason always looked forward to it, ever since they started their daily habit. Angel did not want to admit it to him, but she enjoyed it and looked forward to it just as much.

Nodding off in front of the TV, Angel suddenly opened her eyes, wiped them with the back of her hands, and turned around. "What time is it?" she asked Jason as he entered the house.

"I'm sorry. I'm late again. I should've called you."

"You did call me," she said, yawning. "You called me late in the afternoon."

Jason had stopped on his way home to buy her a box of candy. He was planning to give it to her as he walked inside the house, but suddenly he froze in their kitchen.

"What're you holding in your hand?" she asked.

"I don't know if this will excuse my being late, honey," he said sheepishly and hesitated to finish what he was going to say. "I brought you something." He was very hungry and could smell the aroma of homemade spaghetti, another one of his favorite foods. But he wanted to delay the self-gratification of eating. *Please don't ask me if I am hungry. I feel awful about being late,* he thought.

Angel jumped to her feet, walked to the kitchen, and grabbed the bag out of Jason's hand. She took the box of candy out of the bag and stared at it excitedly. "This is for me?"

"Like I said." He looked at her bashfully, as if the box of candy was not a worthy present for her. "I brought you something."

She hugged him and kissed him passionately. "I love you! I *love* candy. Would you like to have dinner? *I'll eat with you.*"

"I smelled it as I walked inside. Have you eaten yet?" he asked.

"No, I have not. I've been waiting for you." She looked at him with a little bit of guilt. "I tried my best to stay awake."

"I *love* to have dinner with you!"

"Wait! Let me have a candy first." Quickly, she tore up the wrapping paper. As much as she liked candy, as eager as she was to gobble up the entire assortment, she restrained herself. Slowly and deliberately, she took a candy out of the box and put it in her mouth. She let her taste buds enjoy the sweetness and savory taste of chocolate.

Jason noticed the joy and thrill in her eyes immediately. *Oh, my God! She looks like she is in heaven.* He had bought her cakes and flowers, but he did not remember the last time he had bought her a box of candy. *I should buy her a box of candy every night.* Suddenly he could feel and understand what *she* felt watching him eat dinner every night. *That's why she looks at me the way she does at dinner time, every night! How could I have been so stupid?*

That night, Angel finished her meal. Her plate was not quite as full as Jason's, but she finished it all.

Snuggling, they watched their favorite show on TV. Soon, they were in bed. As Jason was about to toss and turn once again, she put her head on his arm and closed her eyes. Jason wanted to do what he had been doing every night, but something was changed and nothing could justify what he was about to do. *It is not right. It is insane! I can't just get out of the bed because of my insomnia. I just can't! I should not!* He suddenly realized that no soft whispering, no post coital special touch, no gentle hug, and no passionate kisses, could excuse what he was about to do. "I am so sorry," he whispered to Angel.

"Why, honey?" she asked in a gentle voice.

"I know you want to go to sleep on my arm. This is the least I can offer you. You should be doing it *every night*."

"Honey, you have insomnia! You can't blame yourself for it. It's not *your fault*." She did not want him to feel guilty; she was trying to soothe him. But she did not want him to leave her either. She wanted him to stay in bed—by her side. She did not want to be in bed by herself. She never did. Jason was right. She wanted to go to sleep on his arm. *Every night.*

AN ANGEL WITH BROKEN WINGS

SUSAN WAS SITTING on the chair and reading a new children's book when John walked into the living room.

"Is that one of the books that your mother bought for you, Princess?" John asked.

"I've already read them, Daddy. This is another one. We borrowed it from the library yesterday. This is another children's book." Susan replied. "What's in *your* hand? What're *you* reading, Daddy?"

"It's another one of Tom Clancy's. Would you like to read it after I'm done?"

Susan responded silently with a polite and definite no. She smiled and shook her head.

Then she said, "Sit next to me, Daddy. We'll read together."

Mary was watching them from the kitchen, through the large open space above the kitchen sink. She looked at John and they had the identical thought. It was something they had talked about many times.

As a child, Susan used to sit on her father's lap, in the very same chair. No one could separate them. As a grown woman, she could not do it anymore. That was an unfair and cruel rule, Susan always thought, and could not understand its necessity. But she had to abide by it. Still, that chair was her domain, her ultimate center of love and serenity. She was not going to give it up so easily.

When Susan was a child, her doctors told Mary and John that she had a low IQ and would be considered mildly retarded. The diagnosis, as painful as it was, made the family much closer, and those precious moments on the chair were irreplaceable for Susan and John. Mary had witnessed and shared the joy of pure and unconditional love between father and daughter. But now, everything was changed. Every time Susan sat on that chair, Mary and John wondered if the chair and its strong connection with the old sweet memories were holding her back from growing to her full potential.

Susan had read one of her father's books, written by Tom Clancy. As an avid reader she appreciated adult books, but she insisted on reading children's books. She retained her baby speech around her parents, when they had no guests, but she spoke with good diction and better than most adults, most of the time. There were times, John and Mary wondered if the doctors were wrong about Susan's diagnosis and wanted to blame the chair for everything. They wanted to persuade Susan to sit in a different spot to read her books, a goal that seemed unattainable.

"You love Daddy's chair, don't you?" Mary said.

John noticed immediately. Susan's relaxed body suddenly stiffened and she squeezed the armrests, holding on to the chair and not letting go. "It's okay, honey. Princess and I can share the chair. We just want to sit next to each other," he told Mary.

"You see, Mommy. Daddy doesn't mind."

Mary wanted to take back her words, but it was too late. She could not look at her daughter and lowered her head. After a short and painful pause, Mary tried to made amends to her daughter. "Susan, honey, Daddy has bought your favorite ice cream. Would you like to have some?"

"Really!" Susan said excitedly. "Banana split, Daddy?"

"Now, sweetheart. Please don't have more than a cup. You'll ruin your appetite. I'm cooking your favorite food."

"You heard it, Daddy? We're having homemade fried chicken and French fries. You heard it, Daddy? Can I help, Mommy? Can I? Please!"

"No, honey. You'll burn yourself. You just sit next to Daddy and read your book."

"Are we eating at the dining table?" Susan asked.

"That's up to you and Daddy."

"Daddy, Daddy. Can we? Can we, please?"

"Okay, Princess. You'll sit on the Princess

chair and I'll sit next to you."

Their dining table could be extended and accommodate up to ten people. When Susan was much younger, they used to invite guests over. They pulled out the sides of the table, and put the leaf in between. Susan always insisted on helping her father. That was years ago, before John brought the leaf to the attic—for good. Mary and John did not invite friends to their house anymore. Susan was not rude or loud. Occasionally she made a comment that was a bit untimely, but she was shy and quiet most of the time. Her parents realized—a long time ago—that not everyone could appreciate her condition and sympathize with her. Just one inept look or remorseful glance could devastate their daughter. She was perceptive and sensitive, which also sparked a doubt concerning her diagnosis.

"Can we make the table big, Daddy? Can we?" Reminiscing, she had her baby tone.

"Princess, I don't know where the leaf is," John said.

"But, Daddy!"

"I don't think we have it anymore, Princess."

Daughter and father were reading and Mary was cooking in the kitchen. She craned her neck and looked at Susan. *I know that white-coated young man will fuss at me. But what do doctors know? They are not God! Right now I don't give a damn about cholesterol! I just want to have a good time with my daughter.*

"Do you need any help, honey?" John asked Mary.

"Not quite yet. Susan will help me set the table when the food is ready. You just read your Tom Clancy book."

Susan did not say anything. She was trying to read, but her mind was on food. Even her favorite ice cream was not a match for homemade fried chicken and French fries.

"Can we go to a movie theater, Daddy?" Susan asked after they finished eating dinner.

"Princess, we had a different plan for tonight," said John.

"We're doing something better, something more fun than watching movies, sweetheart," said Mary.

Earlier in the day John and Mary had a serious conversation about that night. She had suggested the restaurant at the casino. They had been there once. It was a buffet, and formal dress was not required. The food was outstanding and Susan had ice cream twice. "She had so much fun!" Mary kept telling John to persuade him.

"But we can't afford it. It was just too expensive!"

"It was cheaper than a restaurant!"

"It sure was. But still. We're not using credit cards anymore."

"What about a movie theater?"

"We can't afford that either. All I have is my emergency twenty-dollar bill. The one you gave me a long time ago."

"You still have that money? I had completely forgotten about it. That was so long ago."

For a moment John felt good about

keeping his promise to his wife by not spending the money, but nothing could distract him from thinking about his daughter, Susan. He sighed and said, "We just have to stay home and watch TV."

"We haven't taken her out for a long time. We have to do something! Something fun! We owe it to her!"

John knew exactly where Susan wanted to go. She wanted to see her sister Linda more than anything else in the world, and it would have cost them nothing. He thought about the last time he visited Linda. Everything that had happened there flashbacked; as if he were watching a movie, the words were exact and clear. Their son-in-law had just bought a new house and wanted to show it off to him. "We got rid of our old and obsolete furniture, Dad. I am going to build a jungle gym for this little monster," he was telling John and stroking the grandson's hair. "The next thing would be a swimming pool for my princess." They sat down on the new furniture. John was elated to hear that his son-in-law was such a good provider, until his grandson whispered in his mother's ear, "I'm scared of Aunt Susan. She looks weird."

Linda took her son outside discreetly. On the patio, she told him, "Your Aunt Susan is my sister. She *is not* weird. She's *just different*."

John could not hear them. But he could see their body language, and he saw her dilemma. It was painful to watch. But it was more painful for John to think about Linda's feeling toward Susan. *Why doesn't she ever come to see her? Susan is her sister, and she always asks about Linda. Why? Why? Is she embarrassed by her own sister?*

John could not sleep well that night. He thought about the day Susan was born. Everything that had happened then flash-backed. Linda kept asking, "Can I hold my baby sister? Can I? Can I, Dad? Can I, Mom?" She was the most loving and caring sister when Susan was a baby. She wouldn't let anyone else babysit her sister. "Susan is *my* baby sister! She is *my* responsibility!" John had heard Linda saying those exact sentences so many times, so long ago. But somehow, some time ago—John did not remember when—things had changed. *Does Linda think Susan is weird too? For Pete's sake! They are sisters! They are flesh and blood! God! Please let it not be! Why doesn't she come to our house to see her sister? Why doesn't she invite Susan over?* John never shared his tormenting thoughts with Mary and thanked God for the fact that she was not there to see what he had witnessed.

Mary noticed John was holding back something and she pressed for an answer. "You're very quiet. You're scratching your forehead. What's on your mind?"

Should I tell her? No! I cannot! She doesn't have to know. She doesn't need to feel my pain.

"Tell *me!* What're you thinking?" Mary demanded.

"I'm just brainstorming. You're right, we have to do something fun. We owe it to her," John said and proposed a compromise plan. He suggested taking Susan to the casino and giving her his twenty dollars to play the slot machines for fun.

"Are you crazy? You want to take our daughter to a casino and ask her to gamble."

"Just hear me out, honey. Our daughter does her baby talk when no one is around. She is not peculiar. She talks better than most people when we have a guest. She is just shy and quiet. For the most part, she is a normal person." After a short pause he continued. "Those people at the casino go there to become millionaires overnight. They don't care about anybody else. They won't even notice us. Besides, we will be with her." He was thinking hard to make a solid argument, but everything he was saying was also making a lot of sense. He was persuading himself and his wife—at the same time. They both knew Susan deserved to experience a normal life. She was entitled to have fun just like everybody else, even if it was for a short period of time.

John remembered the one and only time they visited the casino. The line for the buffet was too long and they were advised to spend ten to fifteen minutes at the casino. When they walked in the casino, Susan brightened up. She could not keep her eyes off the bright lights that were flashing at the top of the slot machines. She was in fantasy land.

Mary listened carefully and made one weak objection. "What if she wins some money?"

"Good for *her*! I hope she *will*! This may be the gentle push she needs to come out of her cocoon."

"Okay. I have two tens and a five. You hang on to your emergency money, and I will give you my tens, but that will be it. And we'll not take her to the casino again. Agreed?"

"Absolutely! And once inside the casino, we won't leave her *side*."

"What is more fun than movie theaters?" Susan did not have a baby tone.

"We're going to the casino, sweetheart."

"The casino?" Susan immediately remembered their only visit there. She was dazzled by the atmosphere inside. She was not sure if she wanted to go back there again, but there was a strong sense of curiosity that she could not resist. She also could not forget the buffet, the ambience, and the food. *They had the best ice cream.* She was ready to go to the casino.

"Would you look at her! She is sound asleep, like a baby," said Mary, as they were driving to the casino.

"I see her through the mirror. She is holding Mr. Teddy."

"I wish your mother was here to see this. Your mother bought that teddy bear for Linda. Do you remember?"

"Do I remember? Linda *did not* let anyone touch Mr. Teddy as long as my mother was alive. And after her death, she did not want to have it anymore because it reminded her of Grandma Betty, and made her sad. Susan wanted to have Mr. Teddy because Grandma Betty had gone to heaven and she could remember her by holding Mr. Teddy. And you tell *me!* Who was the smart one?"

Mary looked at Susan again. "My baby. She's sleeping so peacefully," she said in her gentlest voice. Then she became silent and remembered painful old memories.

As a toddler, Susan seemed to be too playful and a little bit disobedient. On her fourth birthday she broke one of the most precious things they owned, an expensive and irreplaceable heirloom, a present from John's mother. This was an agonizing and regrettable recollection. She was angry at Susan. She was very angry. She kept repeating, "My precious vase!" She wanted to punish Susan for breaking the vase. She had warned her so many times against swinging the vase.

Neither John nor Linda knew how to react to her unexpected rage.

"Honey, today is her birthday," John pleaded with Mary.

"Do you know how much that thing was worth?"

"Mom! How many times did I break things at her age? She is just a child," Linda pleaded.

A first grader at the age of six, Susan did not seem that much different from any other child, although she struggled with her school assignments from day one. Everyone in the family was patient with her and helped her incessantly.

Six-year-old Susan would lean on her mother and say with watery eyes, "I don't understand it. It is too hard for me."

"I know. It was just as hard for your sister. Learning is never easy," Mary would say and wipe her tears. She would hold her tight and swing her from side to side. "I know, sweetheart. I know."

She remembered Susan at the age of seven. The school principal advised John and Mary to bring her to a child psychiatrist.

"I wouldn't worry too much about it. Her situation is not severe at all. I would not recommend a special school," the psychiatrist told them after reviewing the psychologist's tests.

"But, Doctor! She really struggles. It breaks my heart to wipe her tears. She's just a child. Why can't she be just like her sister?" Mary pleaded with the doctor.

"I'm sorry, ma'am. Doctors are not God. We can't fix everything."

Several doctors reassured them that Susan's condition was very mild. "With a little bit of extra attention, she will do fine and finish high school," they told John and Mary.

"I wouldn't be surprised if she finished college," one of the doctors told them.

At times, some of Susan's classmates were cruel to her. John and Mary talked to her teachers and principal often. Everyone was very supportive, and Linda was the best student at school. Everybody liked Linda, who made sure everyone knew that Susan was her baby sister. When Linda graduated from high school, Susan refused to go back to school. Linda and Mary home schooled her and she passed her GED.

"You're quiet," Mary told John. She did not want to talk. She just wanted to stop thinking about the past.

"I was thinking about Susan," he said and did not elaborate on it. He did not want to talk either. *Why couldn't she be like her sister,*

Linda? She could've lived in her own house. Been a mother! Been a wife! Like her sister! She deserves better! She is my daughter too!

Susan woke up and suspended their agonizing silence. "Mom, could I have ice cream at the casino?"

Mary turned around. "I am sorry, sweetheart. They don't have ice cream inside the casino. They only serve it in the buffet. We just had dinner, sweetheart. I'll get you lemonade, I promise!"

"Okay, Mom," she said. Leaning back, she hugged her only friend, Mr. Teddy.

John parked the car in the garage, and they walked through the lobby. There were several sets of sofas and chairs on the way to the casino. "I want to sit down," Susan said as they were passing by the last sofa.

"What is wrong, Princess? Are you tired?" John asked.

"No. I'm not tired. I just want to sit down."

"Let's sit down then," Mary said and they

sat on the sofa.

There were things that Susan did as a child and she never grew out of them, simple things that children did and adults did not do so often. Sitting between her parents and holding hands was one of them. It brought about her most precious smile.

They sat closely together and Susan leaned on Mary. Then she leaned on John.

You're my angel. Mary thought as they held hands.

"Princess, we love you very much," John said.

"When do we see Linda?" Susan said. "I miss Linda." She sighed. "I miss her, Daddy."

"You'll see her soon, sweetheart. Very soon."

"When? When do we see Linda?"

Susan grabbed John's arm and held on to him as they neared where security guards checked identification cards. Apprehensive, she slowed down her pace and whispered,

"What do I do now, Daddy?"

A man as old as John and a woman about Susan's age were the two security officers. The older man seemed to be in charge.

"Don't be scared, sweetheart," said John. "Don't you remember the last time we were here? They are like police officers. They are here to protect us. We just smile and pass through."

"The young lady must be your daughter, sir. She looks a lot like you," said the older security guard. He had a pleasant demeanor.

"She sure is, and we're very proud of her." After exchanging friendly nods and smiles, John said, "How are you doing tonight, my friend?"

"Just fine, sir. I hope you win." The security guard turned toward Susan. "Young lady, enjoy your visit. I hope you win a lot of money."

Susan held her head down and smiled. She did not say anything.

Susan stopped and looked around as soon as they entered the casino. "Where do we go now?" she asked her parents.

John pulled out a ten dollar bill and said,

"Princess, this is for you. You and your mother find a slot machine that you like. Then you'll put your money in there and start pulling the bar on the side. We'll just watch you, and you'll have all the fun."

"What about you and Mom?"

"We'll be fine. This is your night! We want *you* to have fun tonight."

"That's right, sweetheart. You play and we watch. If you win, the winning money is yours too!" Mary said.

They walked around for a short while. Susan looked really happy. "This one has pictures of animals. I like this one."

"Okay, then. We'll sit here."

Susan sat on the stool quickly. She was grinning and nodding. "Can I?" she asked her parents, holding up her ten-dollar bill.

"Go ahead, sweetheart. Your father gave it to you."

"It's *your* money, Princess."

"I want lemonade, Mom. You promised me!"

"You just sit here, sweetheart. I'll bring you a cup of lemonade."

She held the bar on the side of the slot machine, but did not pull it. "I want to sit by myself, Daddy."

"But, Princess, you promised your mother to stay with us." He was pleading with her.

"Daddy! I want to sit by myself."

John did not want to walk away, but Susan did not appear vulnerable or fragile. She seemed as strong and assertive, as her sister Linda would have been. She was defying everything that the doctors had said about her.

"Okay, Princess. I'll be right there. You just have fun." He walked to a blackjack table not too far away. He was hesitant, but he was also filled with pride and joy. Standing behind the players, he turned his head every now and again and watched Susan having fun effortlessly and confidently. He wanted time to freeze. *There's nothing wrong with my Susan. My daughter is an intelligent woman.*

"What do you think you're doing? We're not here to play blackjack. Where is Susan?

You were supposed to stay with her!" Mary exclaimed.

"Our daughter is just fine," John said calmly, pointing in Susan's direction. "I'm just watching. I'm not playing!"

"But you were supposed to stay with *her*."

"*Look at her! Just look at her!* She'll be fine."

Mary looked at their daughter and grinned. "Are you thinking what I'm thinking?" she asked.

"She's *our daughter!"* John said with a blissful smile.

Just like her husband, Mary wanted everything to stay the way it was. She wanted to watch her daughter having fun. "I'll have to go and check on her quickly. You just stay here. This is for you." She gave him one of the drinks.

"Okay. But don't stay there too long."

Susan had a piece of paper in her hand. She did not seem upset, just a little bit confused.

"Why aren't you playing? What's wrong, sweetheart?"

"What is this, Mom?"

"Let me see." Mary looked at the paper closely. It was a redeemable ticket for twenty dollars. "Who gave this to you, sweetheart?"

"An old lady gave me this. She was very nice and friendly. She reminded me of Grandma Betty."

"Where is she?" Mary asked.

Susan shrugged and did not say anything.

One of the security guards approached them. "What seems to be the problem, ladies?"

Mary showed the ticket to the guard. "Someone left this with my daughter and forgot to come back for it. It's a redeemable ticket for twenty dollars."

"That would be Miss Betty, ma'am. She's just a sweet old lady. If she wins, everyone around her gets some free money."

"Really? Are you sure?"

"I was standing here. Miss Betty *gave* this to your daughter."

"I guess that makes sense now. My daughter tells me the lady was very nice to her, like her late Grandma Betty."

The guard smiled. "Ma'am, Miss Betty is everybody's Grandma Betty."

While John tried to find a trashcan for his empty cup, he lost sight of his wife and daughter. *Where are they? What happened to them?* He noticed them standing at the cashier counter and walked toward them.

"What are you two doing here? Did you win?"

"Daddy, Daddy, some old lady gave me twenty dollars."

"What old lady?"

Mary grabbed his arm. "I'll explain it to you later. Your daughter made twenty dollars and she still has eight dollars of the money you gave her. You go back over there by the blackjack table. I'll be right with you."

"Okay, sweetheart. I'll keep your twenty dollars."

"It's my money."

"Yes, sweetheart. It's all yours and I'll keep it for you, unless you want to play with it."

"Keep my twenty dollars. I want to play with the rest of the money that Daddy gave me. I want to go where the old lady was sitting. She told me, 'This one gives you money.' She was nice to me. She was really kind."

Mary was not sure if her daughter wanted to go back there to see the old lady again or she wanted to play on the lucky slot machine. She did not care either way.

"Okay, sweetheart. Do you remember where she was sitting?"

Susan sat at another slot machine. It was a few stools away from the first one.

"Is this where the old lady was sitting?"

Susan nodded and sat down. She was not talking, but her smile—a smile that did not seem to go away—was saying a lot. It reminded Mary of the old days, when Susan used to snuggle with her Grandma Betty in front of the TV.

"Okay, sweetheart. You just have fun here and I'll sit next to you."

"Please, Mom. I want to sit here by myself. You stay with Daddy."

"Are you sure?"

Susan did not respond verbally. But her look and her body language spoke better and louder than words.

I would do anything to see you smiling like this, Mary thought. "Okay, sweetheart. I'll be right there with your Daddy."

Susan continued pulling on the bar at the side of the slot machine. Every now and then she paused. *Where is the old lady? Where is she?*

Not too far from Susan, John and Mary were standing behind a blackjack table. They were watching other patrons losing their money.

"She'll be fine. She is safe, over there," Mary whispered to John, every time he turned around and glanced at Susan.

The older security guard, the one who had greeted them earlier, was walking by. He stopped and grinned. "Young lady. Are you having fun? Are you winning?"

Susan shrugged. "I don't know. Am I?"

He leaned and said, "Let me show you." His fatherly manner gained Susan's trust. He showed Susan how much money she had in the machine.

"I have fifteen dollars!?"

"That's right. Would you like to cash it out?" He showed Susan which button she could push to get a redeemable ticket.

"I want to play."

When the guard walked away, Susan paused, and looked around. *Should I play? I have fifteen dollars! What if the old lady comes back? Everybody is so nice here*. She turned around and continued pulling on the bar. She had twenty dollars at one point. But she continued playing.

"Are you okay, Princess?"

"I'm fine, Daddy. I still have money," she said, pointing at the digital numbers that indicated the amount of money she had to play with. "You go over there and stay with Mom."

Susan had less than ten dollars and she kept playing. She had less than five dollars and kept playing. Winning was not important to her any more. She just wanted to play. She just wanted to be there. She had two dollars left. Then she had nothing left. She turned around and noticed three women, about her age. They were walking in her direction. They were not frowning. They did not look angry as some other patrons did. They smiled at her and she smiled back. *I'll have new friends.* She relaxed, sat there, and waited for them to get closer. She lowered her shoulders, as they were standing a few feet away from her. She had a bigger smile and expected them to talk to her. But they did not say anything. They just looked at her. They were smiling. But it was a different kind of smile, not the same one as the old lady's, or the friendly guard's. *Why are you looking at me this way? I'm not a monkey! Stop it! Go away!* She wanted to scream at the ladies. *You're not my friends. Just stop it! Just go away!*

The three ladies walked away in less than a minute, but it seemed like an hour of torment to Susan. She sat there after they left. She was not smiling anymore and did not want to talk to anybody. She did not even want to look at anybody in the casino. She wanted the earth to open up and swallow her. She wanted to be anywhere but in that casino. She wanted to die.

"Are you okay, Princess?" John asked.

"Are you okay, sweetheart? What's wrong?"

Mary asked.

Momentarily, Susan looked catatonic. "Can we go home, Daddy? I don't want to be here. Can we go home? Please!"

"What's wrong, Princess? I thought you were having fun!"

"Can we *just* go home?"

"Did you lose your money? You still have another twenty dollars. Do you want the rest of your money?" Mary asked.

"Can we *just* go home?"

Out of desperation, Mary offered to buy her ice cream. "I have five dollars on me. We won't even have to use your money."

Susan was not about to tell her parents why she was so upset. She just wanted to go to the car and hold Mr. Teddy. Mr. Teddy never mocked her. He loved her unconditionally.

Driving home, Mary pulled out the twenty-dollar bill. "This is your money, sweetheart," she said, waving the money with a big fake grin.

"You keep it, Mommy. I don't want it!" Susan held Mr. Teddy tight. Then she closed her eyes and wished to dream of Grandma Betty.

THE MAHARAJA AND HIS PILLARS

John

PACING IN HIS office aimlessly, John stopped in front of each painting on the wall. He stroked his goatee, nodded deliberately, and said, "Picasso, you're my favorite painter. You're a *genius! Just like me!* We belong to a different world. A world made just for the two of us."

Two expensive Chinese vases stood on either side of the entrance door, and an exquisite Persian rug covered the floor. The decoration was an unfinished project. Everything was handpicked by Linda, his previous personal secretary. His new secretary, an exotic dancer one night and a novice secretary the next morning, did not know anything about art collections, nor had she made any attempt to learn. She did not type and could not take notes. The only thing she did was put her feet on her desk and file her nails.

"Keep up the good work, my sweet Rose," John told her every time he walked in. The seductive way he looked at her always betrayed his statement, and he often added, "You get prettier and prettier every time I see you."

Rose, or whatever her name was, always responded by pointing at a provocative item of clothing she wore. "Do you like my new skirt?" She would get up, turn around, and say, "Does it show too much?" She would get closer to him and ask seductively, "I'm wearing a pushup bra. Do you like it?"

"I love it!"

They engaged in this sort of trivial conversation often and John always encouraged her to dress more provocatively. He called her "my sweet Rose" on the first night they met and Rose became her name.

John opened his safe and pulled out a thick stack of hundred-dollar bills. Then he sat on his swivel leather chair with gilded convex pins and threw the bills on his desk. This was an old style chair and the pins were actually gold-plated, but John told everyone that they were "solid gold. Fourteen karat!" Only John and Linda knew the truth.

His hands clipped behind his head, John leaned back and gazed at the top of his mahogany desk. The desk was also handpicked by Linda and he treasured it. Linda used to keep his desk clean and organized. Rose never made an attempt to do it. He wanted to ask Linda to organize his desk, but she was still angry at him for the demotion. Her paycheck was the same, but she had felt betrayed by him. *It's a beautiful desk. I guess I have to get one of the janitors to clean it up for me.*

He started counting the hundred-dollar bills in his money clip. *Should I put any more Ben Franklins in my pocket?* He sighed. *I can never carry a hundred thousand dollars with me. Why do I torture myself like this?*

Soon he felt claustrophobic. He stood

up and started pacing and musing again. He stepped out and told Rose, "Do not let anyone disturb me, for any reason! I have to make a *momentous* decision."

"Yes, Mr. M."

"His first name starts with a J, and his last name starts with a P. Why do you call him Mr. M?" asked another female employee who was sitting by Rose's desk.

Rose shrugged. "I don't know. Everybody calls him Mr. M. Maybe M stands for money."

He walked back inside his office, locked the door, and walked to the wall-size glass window across from his desk. "I am the *Maharaja* and this is my *Taj Mahal*!" he said, as if he was delivering an impassioned speech in front of a large audience. He was looking at the Golden Gate Bridge and thinking about another one of his wild dreams, owning the bridge and replacing it with solid gold.

Shortly after he made his first hundred million dollars, he read about the Caesars of Rome, the Pharaohs of Egypt, the Czars of Russia, and the Maharajas of India. His fascination with Maharajas was due to the legendary Taj Mahal and the priceless jewels they owned, or so he thought.

John Pooldoost was a third-generation emigrant. His grandfather had come to America years ago to become rich.

"Where're we from?" John's father had been asking from the day he could talk.

"Don't worry about where I am from, son," John's grandfather always responded. He took a short pause and added, "You're born in America. You're an American."

Pooldoost literally meant one who loved money, but they had been poor for two generations. The only things that the grandfather had done for them, in terms of fame and wealth, were to leave them a small house, change his first name to John, legally, name his son "John the Second," and insist on naming his grandson "John the Third."

John the Second had been trying to become rich throughout his adult life, as had his father. Over the years, he had made many bad real estate investments, but shortly before his death, he met a man who had genuine talent for real estate investment. Together, they made a few good investments. At the time, everything was in John the Second's name, but both men in their early forties, had agreed to become partners and enjoy their wealth for many years to come. Unfortunately there was a bad automobile accident. The man who hit them was a drunk driver. The parents and the future partner died at the scene of the accident, but John the Third miraculously survived with minor injuries.

He had just finished high school. There was a big lawsuit and a substantial settlement. Being the only child, John the Third became a wealthy citizen overnight. He had inherited the good fortune of his father and a good portion of the settlement. He decided to fulfill his ancestral dream: to become rich, very rich. He paid a professional calligrapher to write his grandfather's frequent advice:

One must live modestly
For quite some time
Before becoming wealthy

Several copies of this calligraphy were framed on the walls inside his ancestral house. He controlled his urges to buy himself expensive watches and jewelry, as any young man in his situation would have done.

Young John found a list of commercial real estate properties that his father and his father's partner had targeted for investment before their demise. He used his share of the settlement, every last penny of it, to purchase as many of these prime real estate properties as he could. As he was becoming a real estate tycoon, he continued living well below his means and invested nearly all his discretional income in prime commercial properties.

Several years after the death of his parents John Pooldoost had more money than he could ever dream. He legally removed "the Third" from his name. He also changed his life story. "I had nothing but a high school diploma when my father ascended to heaven. I've worked hard for everything I own, and I own plenty," he bragged constantly. There was no wife, family, or old friend around to dispute his claim, and to some extent he was right. He had made some sacrifices to be where he was.

Denise

As usual—Denise woke up hungry. "Thank God it is not raining," she said. She tidied up her scant belongings, her only means of comfort and pleasure until now: an old pillow covered with a dirty pillowcase and a tattered blanket. Denise lived in a cavity under the bridge. Looking at an old and rusty bicycle, a present she had received from a Good Samaritan on the previous day, she said, "I don't have to walk anymore. I own a bicycle now!" With measured effort, she picked up her bicycle and examined it thoroughly. "It must've been a beautiful bicycle once. It'll do fine for me."

There were no clouds in the blue sky and it looked as serene and calm as an undisturbed pond from a distance. *This is much better than walking. I just have to find a way of securing my bike when I eat,* the old lady thought. She looked at her bicycle and grinned. *God will look after me and my bike!* She felt her pocket. *And I have a dollar and some change with me.*

In her late forties, Denise Humble thought she had found the light at the end of the tunnel when she met David. He was not a rich man, but he had enough money to pay for his mortgage and the essentials. He also had a modest distrectionary income. He had debt due to his late wife's medical expenses. Truly debonair, David was a kind man, but his children could not accept a replacement for their late mother.

"I'm sorry, my dearest. I'm too old to fight with my children. They're my children, after all. I love you more than you could imagine, but I can't marry you," David told Denise many times when he was alive.

"It's okay, sweetheart. We do everything together. Everyone recognizes us as husband and wife. We have each other and nothing else matters," Denise always replied.

The two of them did not experience romance in a conventional way, but they attended mass together every Sunday. They had a home together, and truly cared for each other. They were lovers of the most simple and genuine kind.

Denise knew it by heart. David was not going to leave her behind and they were going to die in that house together. And so did David. But David died unexpectedly and everything changed. The children kicked Denise out of their father's house, and the house was repossessed by the bank, soon after.

Thomas

After another restless night, Tom dragged himself out of bed. He checked his video on You Tube to see how many new viewers had listened to it overnight, as he did first thing every morning. The audiovisual was a narrated short story. His friends and acquaintances had watched it. They told him it was "a good story," "very interesting," "very intense." One told him, "It touched my heart." Another one told him, "I didn't realize you cared so much about this issue." Just about everyone liked the story, but they all thought the video was boring and repetitious. One close friend even told him, "I loved your story, but the video sucked."

Tom's response was simple and honest. "I learned to write in college, but no one taught me to make movies." He appreciated his friend's frank comment, thanked him for listening to his story, and thought, *I have done something that will last forever and no one can take it away from me*.

Tom had a humble life and lived like an ascetic. He lived with his wife. She had a better job and did not ask anything of him. Several friends and associates read his writing pages at a time and asked for more. Nothing made Tom happier than sharing his gift. He was becoming a prolific writer and that was the most important thing to him and his wife.

A previous employer had let him work overtime, sometimes with no weekends, for many months. That was how Tom had raised the money to finance the construction of the stage for his video. After purchasing an expensive camcorder, he had made many trips to Lowe's, often early in the morning. Laying the back seat down and making it flat, he had carried as many two-by-fours as he could in his wife's old Nissan Altima. He had built the stage by hand with his primitive tools, on his off days. Tom was not a carpenter and he had learned everything by trial and error.

Every morning, as he listened to the beginning of the narration, he reminisced about the old days, on his previous job. That was not too long ago. Then, he woke up in the middle of the night—just about every night—and wrote for hours. *I wish I had my old job. Those good old days! I would've finished my last novel and God knows what else.* He often recalled the comment he had made to a close co-worker. "I've been writing again! I went to bed at nine o'clock this morning and woke up at three in the afternoon. I had just enough time to ride my bike to work. I guess novelists don't have to take a shower every day." At the time, he did not think that he was smelling bad, nor was he embarrassed. He just felt proud and dedicated, and wanted to humor his co-worker.

Tom did not know when and if he was going to get published. Writing, he thought, was a noble thing, and he was not going to give it up. *Ever!*

Some mornings he was sad and thought life was too cruel, but he always put a smile on his face and told himself, *Had it not been for my hard work and determination, I could've never afforded to produce my You Tube video.*

Thomas graduated from UNO in December of 1988. In January, he enrolled in graduate school, studying Business Administration. It was a bad decision and some faculty members tried to talk him out of it. But Tom was scared. *If I can't find a job, I have to go back to school. What else can I do?* He enrolled in the first college that admitted him and ignored, his mentor, a faculty member at the History Department. Now, many years later, Tom was casually walking on the campus, and reminiscing about his past. Somehow he wanted to redeem himself and make up for his past mistakes, but he did not know how.

"Dr. Homer. Do you remember me?" Tom asked his former teacher.

"Of course I do. We all do. Are you a CEO now?"

"Far from it," Tom replied sheepishly. He did not want to be rude, but it was very hard for him to make direct eye contact. "You know that was never my forte. I was just scared."

Dr. Homer nodded and patted his shoulder. "I have to tell you, Tom. You disappointed all of us." He paused and waited for Tom to respond, but Tom was reticent. His former teacher sighed. "MBA. We knew you did not belong there. We all knew it."

Some ten minutes later Tom was in Dr. Homer's office. Like the old days, they were chatting and Tom was talking about his new plans. "I want you to watch my video. A friend has narrated it for me, but it is my story. I wrote it."

They watched the You Tube video together.

"This is really interesting. I didn't know you could write so well."

"Don't you remember the story about the homeless student at the campus? The one on the front page of the school newspaper? The one I asked you to read?"

"That was a very good story. *You wrote that one too?"*

Tom smiled victoriously.

"Why didn't you tell me that you wrote it? *You should've told me*!"

"I couldn't. That was the only way I could persuade the student to talk to me. I had promised not to reveal his identity, or my identity as the reporter." For a moment, Tom felt that he had betrayed his mentor to do his job professionally. He lowered his head and added, "That was the only way I could write the story. I had no other choice, Dr. Homer."

"Tom, you don't owe me an apology for being a professional journalist. I just wish I knew you wrote it." Dr. Homer sighed. "No one knew who wrote that piece. We all thought it was written by a faculty member who did not want to reveal the identity of his student." He sighed again. "Believe me! Had I known this then, I would've found a way to enroll you in graduate school, in the English Department. I would've persuaded you! I wish that I knew it then."

Tom grinned and nodded with joy. "I was

the one who wrote it, and I insisted on remaining anonymous."

"And I always thought you would've become a good history teacher. You fooled me!"

"You always liked my papers."

"I sure did." After a while, Dr. Homer leaned back in his chair. He looked at Tom as if Tom were a visiting faculty member. "When are you going to bring me your autographed novel then?"

"I'm trying Dr. Homer. I'm trying very hard. Do you know how hard it is to get published?"

"It is hard. It's very hard, but I don't want you give up. Promise me you won't mess it up this time."

Richard Watson

A former detective, Richard Watson was promoted to the general manager position for a failing shopping center.

"It is the demographic, Richard," his boss, Sam, had told him many times. He always patted Richard on his shoulder and shook his head in disappointment. "There's nothing we can do about it now. This place has gone to hell in a handbasket." Richard worked much harder than his former boss to revive the business, but fewer and fewer shoppers were coming to the mall, and one by one, the remaining store owners were refusing to renew their rental contracts.

John Pooldoost became the new owner. Originally, the mall had four major department stores, fifty stores from medium to large size, and ten booths and pushcarts. The parking lot could easily accommodate a thousand cars. The selling price for the failing mall was six million dollars! That was a deal John could not walk away from.

"Mr. M, a Richard Watson is waiting on the line for you. He's calling long distance. Says you would like to talk to him," Rose said.

John was still gazing at the Golden Gate Bridge, trying to figure out the cost of replacing the entire bridge with solid gold. *I can have it gold plated and lie about it.*

"Mr. M, Richard Watson is still on line."

Rose said for the third time.

"Put him through."

Richard had practiced being articulate, and concise. He knew "the big boss" expected him to speak sparingly and listen carefully. He made a brief report, as he was asked through a text message. The numbers were not what his new boss wanted to hear. Not even close. Three stores had refused to renew their rental contract and two of them had already left the mall. The only promising news was the cost. He had managed to reduce the cost, once again, without eliminating any essential service to the customers or the merchants.

"That's all you have for me? That's it? I've spent *six million dollars* on that worthless shopping center. When do I get the proper return on my investment?"

"You just acquired it a month ago. And I've already eliminated six positions to make it more profitable."

"Six million dollars and six positions. Sounds good. They rhyme together," he said, interrupting Richard. "So, do you have any good news? Any new ideas?"

"Sir."

John interrupted Richard again. "How about raising the rents? That will bring us more money!" He raised his voice. *"How about it?"*

"We have considered it, sir. But I'm afraid it may not be a good idea. It will create additional vacancies, and that, we simply can't afford right now."

"So, what do you suggest?"

"I'm working on a game plan to attract more shoppers."

"I like that. What's holding you back?"

"We need to review our marketing strategy. We need to advertise more frequently and more efficiently."

John interrupted Richard for the third time. "If this is your pitch to milk more money out of me, forget it! I've already spent enough money on that worthless piece of property! I need more revenue! Raise the rent!" He slammed the phone and instructed Rose not to let Richard through for the rest of the day.

Tom was in his driveway. Holding the handle bars on his bicycle, he was about to leave for work. His immediate neighbor was working on one of his cars. "I should be doing that, Tom. It's a good day to ride a bike."

"Why would you do that? You have two nice cars," Tom responded.

"You know better than that, Tom. My wife drives the newer one."

"So does mine," Tom said, and they chuckled. "We have only one old car and that is hers."

"Say. I watched your video. You can really write. When are you going to write a novel?"

"I have written two! I just can't persuade anyone to publish them."

"How much did you spend on the video? I know you made the stage, but who paid for the material?" the neighbor asked.

"Working overtime and weekends paid for it." Tom did not hold back very much. He was blunt and honest.

"It's not any of my business, but you could've probably bought yourself a reliable car for that money."

"But I want people to read my stories. So far, this is the best I have done."

Tom and his neighbor had known each other for many years. They were good friends, but Tom was not comfortable talking anymore about his income, and they did not have a long conversation.

"My baby! My beautiful bike!" Denise cried out the moment she realized that she had a flat tire. *What am I going to do now? Who'll help me?* She started walking her bicycle on the shoulder of the road. The sunny and delightful day did not seem so pleasant any more. But the old lady was not a quitter. *God will provide*, she told herself, and continued walking her bicycle.

He might have a pump, she thought as Tom approached her.

"I need air in my tire. Do you have a pump?"

Tom could not understand what she was asking for. *I'll be late for work.* He did not want to stop, but seeing her face and body language, he could not just keep riding his bike.

"Do you have a pump?" Denise asked again when Tom stopped.

"I have a pump. Do you have a flat tire?"

"You do have a pump! I'm so glad!"

Tom leaned his bicycle against a tree on the side of the road carefully and brought his tools to Denise's bike. It was easy for him to connect the pump's air tube to the valve stem.

"It looks good now. I have air in my tire now," Denise rejoiced as Tom struggled to disconnect the pump's air tube.

"I would like to help you, but I'll be late for work."

The two of them struggled to disconnect the tube, but it was tightly attached to the valve stem.

She looked desperate. He looked desperate.

"I would like to help, but I can't be late for work," Tom said again and walked a few yards away to pick up a short two-by-two from the side of the road.

"You won't be able to pull it out that way," he told Denise, and hit the connecting part of the pump's air tube with the board.

He managed to disconnect them, but the valve stem fell off, rendering Denise's tire, hence her bicycle, useless.

My bicycle is ruined, Denise thought, but did not complain. *What do I tell him? He had good intentions.*

Tom did not say anything. *What have I done?* They looked at each other for a few seconds. Then Tom pulled out his reserve tube from his homemade duffle bag. "This is my spare tube. You keep it, but I have to go to work."

"I'm sorry if I made you late for work. I have a dollar. Maybe I should give it to you!" Denise said, candidly.

"No! Keep your money and my spare tube," Tom replied, and rode his bicycle to work. Along the way, he thought about turning around and leaving his bicycle pump with the old lady, but he did not. *I'm going to be late for work.*

He arrived at his place of employment

within twenty minutes and was not late at all.

Denise continued walking her bicycle, hoping and praying for a miracle.

It was 8:00 a.m. John Pooldoost had just woken up, after having a bad nightmare. In his dream, he was the Maharaja and the Taj Mahal belonged to him. This was a recurring dream, and once again, he was disgracefully removed from his beloved palace. He wanted to talk to someone about his dream, but he could not think of anybody. *I'm not going to work today*. He called Rose and picked her up. They went to the only store where he purchased his clothes. They were the only ones there.

"Why does every one call you Mr. M, John?" Rose asked.

"I don't know," he replied with a mysterious smile. "Because I'm a magnificent guy! Because I'm marvelous! I was just joking, M stands for something else."

"Does it stand for money?" she asked. She

was very serious.

John smiled fiendishly, and said, "No, it does not!"

"Mr. Pooldoost." A man wearing a dark suit, in his late fifties, was walking toward John as if John were a dignitary. "It's so good to see you, sir." He shook John's hand. He wanted to say this must be your lovely wife, but he knew better. "We've been expecting you for a while now. Are you ready to try your new suit, sir? I think you will like it."

John shrugged and looked like he did not want to be bothered, but the suit was paid for and he wanted to pick it up. He tried on the $7,000 suit.

"It really looks good on you. Is it tailor made?" Rose asked.

He nodded nonchalantly. "I guess. What do we do now?" he asked Rose.

"I don't know. You want me to pick a tie?"

"Why don't we drive over the Golden Gate Bridge?"

"Okay."

Rose had the flirtatious attitude of a dancer. She was undulating as she had done on a dance table, the night they met. As they held hands and walked toward John's Lamborghini, Rose said, "Am I still your sweet Rose?"

John shrugged and did not reply. She looked at him more closely, but his face remained expressionless. *There's nothing there,* she thought.

Tom had a restless night. He was still feeling guilty about leaving the homeless lady stranded on the side of the road. *I had to go to work,* he had told himself many times, but the guilt was there, and he could not forgive himself. *How could I be so cruel and selfish?* He paced in the living room and thought about sharing his anguish with his wife. But he was still ashamed of himself.

"It's kind of cloudy, Tom. Let me give you a ride to work," said Tom's neighbor. Tom paused and stared at his neighbor's car. *Gosh, it would so much easier.*

"It's very tempting Sam, but I don't think so."

"Come on! Don't be stubborn. Let me drive you to work, and your wife will pick you up tonight."

Tom looked at the sky. There were dark clouds everywhere. He shrugged. "Let me put my bike inside first."

"You seem preoccupied, Tom. Do you have something on your mind? Would you like to talk about it?" Sam asked as he drove.

"Something is eating me up. But I'm still not comfortable talking about it."

"Why not? We've known each other for a long time," Sam said.

"I just need time to cope with it. I will tell you. I promise."

"I'll be home tonight. Would you like me to pick you up?"

"It's so kind of you, but my wife will do it, I'm sure."

Sam wanted to insist. He did not want to see his friend so disturbed. *Tom will be Tom. He'll tell me when he's ready.* "Okay, buddy. You know where I am."

Looking at the dark clouds, Denise wrapped her tattered blanket around herself. She was hungry, but she wanted to go back to sleep and dream of her late husband again. In her dream they talked about the previous day. She told him about the flat tire and everything else. He listened to her. He smiled, and it was the same loving and caring smile. It was as if he was alive and they lived in their house again. "What happened after the man left you with your flat tire?" her husband had asked. Denise woke up before she could answer. She wanted to go back to sleep and tell her late husband the rest of the story. She wanted to tell him what she did with the spare tube. "I need to go back to sleep," she whispered to herself. But the sky looked too menacing. "I can't! I just can't. What if it rains?"

ON THE SHOULDER OF AIRLINE HIGHWAY

THE FOUR BLINDS on the windows facing their backyard were all the way down, but at seven in the morning some light was coming through the shades and the living room was bright enough for Bret to see everything. He stood there and looked around. Yawning, he moved his shoulders back, clasped his hands behind his neck, and stretched his shoulders further back. Momentarily, he wanted to suspend all thoughts. He wanted to be in the world of nothingness and envied his wife Sylvia for sleeping so peacefully in their bed.

Today was her day off, but almost always he woke up before she did.

He scowled at the blue curtain that covered their large sliding glass patio door, on the side of the room. *I wish she would let me buy a new curtain. Anything but this!* The insulated synthetic drape, resembling cotton fabric, was worn out. Bret did not have the money to buy a new curtain, but he had mentioned it many times and his wife always shot him down quickly.

"You know we can't afford to buy a new curtain. For Pete's sake! You're fifty-five years old and ride a bicycle to work every day."

"We own *a car!* I'm perfectly happy to ride my bike. You need to drive the car."

Their Nissan Altima was fifteen years old. It had several dents and faded paint. But it was reliable and had all the luxuries Bret expected of a car. The windows were automatic and all could be controlled from the driver's seat. The AC was working fine and the car had a radio and a CD player. Even the side mirrors could be adjusted from the inside. The fabric on the seats was worn, but the seats were very comfortable. Bret had never owned a luxury car and could not imagine having any other gadgets in a car. For all he cared, he was driving a brand-new Mercedes-Benz every time he drove their car. Sylvia always worried about him riding his bicycle on the shoulder of Airline Highway. She wanted them to share the car, but their working schedule was very different and she did not wake up on her own to give him a ride to work.

It's time to go to work, Bret thought. But instead of getting ready, he turned around and stared at the wall across from the patio door. A brick fireplace with a wooden mantel was at the center of the wall. Two white marble vases, one on each side, stood on the mantel, with several framed pictures in between them. Two wall-imbedded library shelves on the sides of the fireplace were filled with books, mostly classic literature. Bret and Sylvia were both well educated, but they had acquired very little wealth—other than what Bret was staring at. Their wall in their living room transcended the entire house, and made him forget about their obsolete furniture.

He took his eyes off the bookcases and looked at the sofa. On the previous night, after riding his bicycle home from work, a six-mile-ride, he had collapsed on the sofa and Sylvia had massaged his shoulder. The feeling of joy and comfort, a total submission to pleasure and relaxation, a complete serenity that made him momentarily at ease with the world, was still fresh in his mind.

Most of the jobs Bret had held since graduate school were harsh and dehumanizing. Those with GEDs considered such jobs beneath them, but Bret accepted those jobs and kept his resentment private. Most people perceived his silence as an admission of defeat. They thought he had given up fighting and accepted his fate a long time ago, long before he met Sylvia.

Bret always drove Sylvia to the drugstore and took her to the doctor's office. They went to the grocery store together, at least once a week, and he always paid utility bills in a timely manner. Nothing was more important to Bret than having a steady source of income. The husband and wife were always together and no one had seen them arguing.

No one realized, but Bret was struggling internally. What he called his "morning reflection" was his daily exercise of coping with life. Every morning he reminded himself how lucky he was to have such a caring and giving wife. Every morning he told himself that he had to bear another day of working an unfulfilling job. He had spent many sleepless nights in college to prepare himself for a meaningful career, and his belated dream was never forgotten.

Bret walked into a smaller room. His bike was leaning against the wall, next to a homemade duffle bag, filled with a bicycle pump and a few bicycle tools. "We need some air in those tires, don't we?" he said, and pulled out the air pump. He did not mind talking to himself when no one was around. It was a habit that he had inherited from his father.

He looked at the rain suit at the bottom of the duffle. A while back, Sylvia had purchased it for him. "I don't have any room in my duffle bag for a rain suit. I only have enough room for my pump and my tools," he had protested stubbornly. But, in the end, he had lost this battle too, and the rain suit had become an essential part of his traveling bundle.

Before leaving for work, it was his daily habit to look out the window. A brief hesitation always took place at the sight of bad weather. *Should I drive the car?* Bret was aging faster than he realized, and riding his bike always brought him fresh memories. He was still young in his mind. *It never stopped me when I was in college. I did it throughout graduate school. I'm going to ride my bike!*

Old age and a harsh life had partially drained his soul, but Bret had remained resilient, and riding his bicycle had helped him to retain his spirits.

After walking out of the bathroom, he looked at the sky again, pulled the rain suit out, and looked at it. "Sylvia was right. You may come in handy today." Quickly, he put everything back inside, reorganized and closed the duffle, and started preparing his breakfast. As always, this was the most elaborate daily meal for him, a banana, a bowl of oatmeal, and two scrambled eggs.

"There we go! Bishop is at it again," he said as he was preparing to leave the house. "Bishop" was their immediate neighbor. His house was not much bigger than the surrounding ones, but his lawn was flawless. He had the largest, healthiest, and best-looking pruned holly hedges in front of his house, and one could see them from hundreds of yards away. He mowed and edged his grass often. Everything was always green, lush, and manicured. Once a police officer, he had graduated from a seminary college a long time ago. He was the pastor of a small church, some fifteen miles away from his house.

Several years ago, Bret had become unemployed. He was desperate and the Bishop found him a job, as a cashier, in the mall.

As soon as Bret walked out the door, the Bishop gave him his special look, and said, "Heading for work, Bret?" Bret knew exactly what the Bishop was thinking. *You should be retired. You should be driving a Cadillac, not this flimsy bicycle*. Several months ago, on one sunny Saturday, he had told Bret casually, "You should be playing golf today. It's such a lovely day." Bret was heading to work on his bicycle on that day too. He smiled and did not respond verbally.

"That's why your house is so beautiful, Bishop. You won't give up. Not even on a day like this."

"Oh no! I'm done, Bret. Do you need a ride to work? It's kind of cloudy."

Bret softly tapped on his duffle bag. "I'm ready for it, Bishop. Sylvia has bought me a rain suit."

The Bishop wanted to insist on his offer, but he recognized the smile on Bret's face. He knew Bret was determined to ride his bicycle to work and a monsoon could not hold him back.

"Just be careful."

"I will, Bishop. Thank you so much for the offer." Bret nodded and jumped on his bike.

"Any time, Bret. Any time."

The Bishop's two young granddaughters, his daughter, and his wife, knew Bret very well. On a few occasions, Bret had tutored the grandchildren. They all loved and respected him. But they too had a nagging question mark in their heads. *Why can't he do better than this?*

The first mile was the easiest part of the daily trip for Bret. He rode his bike in the neighborhood and on the sidewalk. He did not carry on a conversation with any of the neighbors. They didn't know Bret and Bret did not know them. Bret often wondered what they thought of him riding a bicycle to work every day.

A lanky man, much older than Bret, sat on a folding metal chair, in front of his house. They waved at each other every morning. The old man had a benevolent smile and they exchanged a "good morning" daily.

Bret's own sister was very critical of everything he did. She was embarrassed by him. "Why don't you buy your shirts from a decent store at the mall? That's why you can never find a good job."

Once Bret turned left on Airline Highway and started riding on the shoulder, it became a dreadful experience. Not too long ago, a negligent truck driver veered off the road and drove on the shoulder of Airline Highway for a few hundred yards; he ran over a road sign with his full size pickup truck. There was so much uproar and disturbance that merchants ran to the street to see what was going on. The truck had bent the sign, but the metal fender did not seem to be damaged. As Bret witnessed, the driver stopped the truck, walked over to the sign, walked back to his truck, and drove away. He was lucky on that day. The man was driving a good distance behind him. From that day on, he rode his bike against the traffic.

Today, Bret had decided to break his own rule and drive with the traffic again. He wanted to break the monotony of his daily trip.

There it goes. Another eighteen-wheeler! The smog and the road dust that the big trucks delivered in his face as they zoomed by were quite unbearable.

Bret had divided his trip on Airline Highway in three different sections, mentally and visually. Thinking about the first two major traffic intersections made him pedal harder and faster, and the third one indicated his arrival at the mall.

It was somewhere close to the second major intersection on this particular day that Bret noticed something amazing. A malnourished middle-aged woman was traveling with a four-wheel cart on the shoulder of Airline Highway. The wheels under the cart did not touch the ground at ninety-degree angles. One of the wheels had a damaged bearing. It was stuck and did not rotate at all. She switched her position from walking behind the cart to the side of it. Crushed beer and soft drink cans were packed inside the cart—to the rim. She pushed, pulled, and occasionally dragged her pile of treasure. A rusted radiator, damaged beyond repair, was laid flat on the shelf under the cart. A valuable part of her treasure, the radiator had made the cart even heavier. She had a constant visual inventory of the cans, but as for the radiator, she had to bend over every now and then to make sure that it had not fallen out and been left behind on the side of the road.

From a short distance, Bret saw her

gasping for air several times. He saw everything—and did not notice anything—as did the commuters.

"You big monster! I'll take you there. You know I will! I'm more stubborn than you are," the woman whispered, whenever she could catch her breath. Her frailty had not compromised her determination, and—somehow—her vulnerability had made her stronger. "I'll take you there. You *know* I will!"

As Bret passed by her, he said, "Good morning!" with a big smile.

The woman just smiled. It was a fake smile. *What is so good about it? I am exhausted! I am hungry! I'm__*

They exchanged a brief and intense glance. For a second—just a brief second—Bret saw and noticed *everything*. He noticed her forced expression, her anguish, her plea for help—and a lot more.

My gosh! What determination! How long has she been collecting those cans? There're so many of them! And that's all she has to her name. This is more than a job. A lot more!

The woman wanted to leave her cart

behind, stop Bret, and grab him by his collar. *Don't you see my anguish? Can't you feel my pain?* She was angry. At the same time, she knew Bret had no contempt for her—in spite of his incredible naiveté. She wanted to present her case to him. For her, it was not about winning the war. She wanted to stand her ground and fight a battle with Bret. *My gosh! It feels so good. It feels so good just to think about it. I want to stand up to him! Her eyes followed Bret as he padeled in opposite direction. I have to tell him like it is! I have to tell him I wasn't always homeless. I have to tell him I was just like him, and it wasn't too long ago. I have to tell him! I just have to!*

She paused. *I could never catch up with him.* She looked at him enviously. *Look at the way he is pedaling. And look at me! I better stay with my original plan. The recycling center is not too far away.* She also had assigned certain intersections and buildings as markers to ease her navigational ordeal. She too could track her movement, visually and mentally. And now, she could see the recycling place.

The old man will be there! I'm sure of it!

He has to be there! She did not know anything about "the Old Man," nor did she know his name. He was just another employee at the place, the one who had assessed her recycling commodity on her last visit. She was convinced that he would give her, twenty dollars, at the very least. *He smiled at me. He talked to me. Really, really talked to me! He looked at me! We had direct eye contact!* She took another visual inventory of her recycling treasure, as she was a few steps away from her final destination. *I could only buy me a hamburger last time. I'll buy small French Fries—with my hamburger—this time.*

KINDERGARTEN GRADUATION

This story is dedicated to Kaitlynn.

EVERY MORNING AT seven, Russell walked to his daughter's bedroom before going to work. He always stroked her hair and gave her a gentle kiss on the forehead. Jennifer always woke up when her father kissed her. Sometimes it was his hesitation at the threshold; other times it was the smell of his aftershave, or the delicate tickling of his mustache against her face. As much as young Jennifer expected and relished this tender act of love, she pretended to be sleeping most mornings. She knew her father would have felt guilty about waking her up so early every morning. Occasionally, she kissed Russell and told him, "I love you, Dad."

It was 8:30 a.m. Jennifer was tossing and turning in her bed. She did not have to go to kindergarten this morning. Under any other circumstances, she would be enjoying sweet dreams after receiving the delightful morning present from her father. It was neither the distinctive aroma of her mother's homemade pancakes, nor the sizzling sound of breakfast sausage that was keeping her up. Young Jennifer was thinking about the previous day. She could not understand why it was her mother's responsibility to go to her classmates' parents—one by one—and collect their crayon artwork for today.

She had asked, "Why can't the other moms bring it to school?"

"It's not that they don't care about their children, sweetheart," Donna told Jennifer. "Some moms just have more free time."

Jennifer smiled and did not respond, but she was not convinced. Miss Susan, the kindergarten teacher, had given a note to every child in the classroom days in advance, requesting the parents bring the best artwork for this event.

It was 9:00 a.m. Other than Donna, Jennifer, and their adorable and playful bichon frise, there was no one else in the house. The small canine was sitting on the chair next to Jennifer, wagging her tail.

A stack of pancakes was in front of Jennifer. Cut in eight equal wedges and saturated with syrup, the pancakes were half consumed. Jennifer could never eat more than two pancakes, but she always insisted on having four. Donna had a feeling that she was going to eat all her pancakes this morning. There was a small bowl of fresh strawberries next to Jennifer's plate. She also had two sausages on her plate. She had given two small pieces of sausage to Penny, their dog, while Donna was in the kitchen. Donna did not like Penny to beg for food, nor did she like Jennifer to give her any, but they were incorrigible.

"Mom, did Penny eat?" Jennifer asked.

"Penny ate this morning, while you were in bed."

"She looks at me. Can I give her a sausage?"

"No honey. That's for you. Penny had plenty of food this morning."

"But she looks at me, Mom."

"I know honey. She loves you."

"Mom, Penny is my baby sister. I have to stay with her. She'll miss me."

"She'll be fine, sweetheart. She has plenty of toys and Daddy took her for a walk this morning. Finish your food. And please don't give Penny any more of your sausage. I have to call your teacher."

"Why?" Jennifer asked.

"We have to go to school. I have to help Miss Susan and Principal Williams."

"Why?" Jennifer asked again. "I thought we were going there this afternoon." She could not understand why her mother was doing so many things that other mothers should, but would not do.

"Sweetheart, we have to hang the artwork on the walls. We have to prepare the classroom for this afternoon," Donna said with a winsome smile. She kneeled and held Jennifer's face with both hands. "We're going to decorate your classroom. So you'll remember it forever." She kissed her, "This is an important day for you, for all of us, sweetheart. We *will* remember it for a long time."

The janitor had moved the small tables and chairs by the time Jennifer and Donna arrived at the classroom. The cubicles were organized. All teaching tools, big numbers and alphabet letters, were organized and stacked neatly. There was nothing on the floor. Games and children books were on the bookshelf.

"Jennifer and I have brought a few things to decorate the room," Donna said and put a box on the bookshelf.

Principal Williams looked at Jennifer and smiled. Jennifer had seen the same smile before. It was right after the last PTA meeting. She overheard her father talking to her teacher. "You know my parents have given Donna a nickname. They call her 'full-time do-gooder.'

She can't stop doing community work." Her father could not—did not—conceal his pride.

That night, Jennifer saw the same smile on her teacher's face. "We all feel the same way about your wife. I don't know how she manages to do so much. But God bless her," Miss Susan told Russell.

The very next morning Miss Susan was waiting for Jennifer outside the classroom. She smiled and stroked Jennifer's hair. "There she is! My little angel! My little-do-gooder! I wish I had more students like you."

Jennifer did not want to be called "little-do-gooder." She was not sure how her classmates would react to it.

"What is this soft bag in the bottom of the box?" Miss Susan asked. She became quiet immediately and looked at Principal Williams frantically. She could see a pink T-shirt through the transparent bag, the one that was purchased for Jennifer.

Donna turned toward Susan and said, "What soft bag?" as Jennifer walked toward Miss Susan.

Principal Williams realized quickly what

was about to happen.

Jennifer was very curious and too smart for her age; she would have figured it out, just by looking at the bag. Miss Susan, Principal Williams, and Donna had worked together to find the T-shirt for her and it was going to be a surprise gift.

Principal Williams walked faster than Jennifer toward Miss Susan and grabbed the box quickly.

"I'll take it to my office. I don't want anyone else to see it." She looked at Donna with pretend disappointment. "I love you, Donna. But you know better than doing this. You were not supposed to bring it here. It's an adult thing."

"I'm sorry, Principal Williams. I don't know how it ended up in that box. I hope it's the right size."

"I'm sure it is, Donna," said Principal Williams. "Do I owe you any more money?"

"Oh, no. Everything is fine. You just take it to your office and we'll talk about it later."

Susan and Donna were staring at the walls when Principal Williams returned from her office with the box in her hand. "So what do you think? Do we have enough room for the artwork?"

"We were thinking about the same thing," replied Donna. "It'll be a challenge, but we'll manage. I have to go back to the car and bring the artwork."

"Good idea. In the meantime, I think we should reward Jennifer. Don't you think?" she said, looking at Susan and Donna. "Would you bring Jennifer to the cafeteria? I'm sure Barbara has some cookies and milk, maybe ice cream too."

Donna had to make two trips, and Miss Susan helped her on the second one, to bring the artwork.

"You're an angel, Donna. How did you manage to collect them all?" asked Principal Williams.

"Believe me! It was not easy," Donna replied, chuckling. "Not to mention the instructions I received from some of the parents." She paused. "Paige's mother told me 'I'll sue you if my daughter's artwork is not the first one to be noticed.'"

"Welcome to the club. She wants to sue everybody," said Susan.

"Who else gave you a hard time?" asked Principal Williams.

"Oh, one of the fathers told me, 'You better put my son's name under his artwork. I don't want any other kid getting credit for his artistic talent.'" Chuckling, she added, "He was so kind. He did not threaten me with a lawsuit."

They laughed.

"I know that father. He's working on his GED and thinks no job is good for him," said Principal Williams.

Ten boys and five girls, all the same age, were standing in a line at the back of the room. Every now and then one of the children giggled, moved back a little bit, and asked, "Is she looking?"

"She is now" was the response by another

student, while Miss Susan gestured for the mischievous child to move back into the line.

"We're going to have ice cream. My mom told me," one of the boys whispered to the girl next to him.

The girl whispered something back. Then they laughed and made funny faces at each other.

There was some harmless poking and discreet laughter. For the most part, the children stood in line obediently.

Two of the boys wore white shirts, black suits, and black bow ties, as if they were ring bearers in a wedding ceremony. Two other boys wore dark blue and dark brown suits, with ties. They too looked just as spiffy. Everybody had worn their best clothes. With fresh haircuts, they all looked very Christmasy. One of the girls had pigtails, and two had ponytails. The rest of the girls, including the two who were standing in front of the line, had their straight and silky hair combed back, about two inches below their shoulders.

Jennifer and Paige were standing in front of the line. They both looked very nervous.

Paige had distanced herself from Jennifer. She had also stepped back, a little bit. Paige's mother was gesturing to her daughter to move forward, but Paige was ignoring her.

Aside from the teacher and principal, there were seventeen mothers and several fathers in the room. With the exception of Paige's mother, they all looked delighted to be there.

"Two of our girls, Jennifer and Paige, have volunteered to be the mistresses of our ceremony. They have a few words to say, before we give out the certificates," announced Miss Susan.

Everybody in the room clapped when the principal gave them the cue.

"Come closer, sweetheart," Paige's mother said loudly.

Who are you? other parents thought, looked at the mother with raised eyebrows.

Jennifer read the paper in her hand. Prepared by Miss Susan, it was suitable for a smart and articulate five-year-old child. Jennifer had the best diction. She was also the only student who was willing to read the statement, with some persuasion. Donna, a homemaker and community activist, was there with her husband.

Paige's father was not present. Shortly before the event, Paige's mother had called him as he was entering the courtroom. "You have to be here for your daughter. She only graduates from kindergarten once." She was screaming at him on the phone. "You just have to be here."

"Honey, I am the defense attorney. I can't tell the judge in the middle of the trial, sorry, I have to leave. My daughter is graduating from kindergarten."

"Why don't you ask for change of venue? Then you will be here."

"It's called a motion. No! I cannot ask for a motion for this." He hung up the phone as she was screaming at him.

Paige wanted to stand in the back of the room with the rest of her classmates. Her mother was the only one who had insisted on this. "If you don't make my daughter the mistress of ceremony, I will have my husband sue you." She had threatened the teacher and school principal several times. Her husband was a senior partner at a medium-size law firm. They knew her word was good. Her husband had to abide by her demand.

"Sweetheart, you'll make your mother very happy. Besides, Jennifer needs you. She is your best friend. She'll be very nervous if you do not stand next to her. She'll be reading. You just have to stand up there and be pretty," the teacher had told Paige several times to persuade her.

The whole ceremony did not take more than an hour, as it was planned. The kids were yawning toward the end. But the parents looked arrogantly proud.

"Did you see what she was wearing? And she is supposed to be a community activist."

"Would you believe it? She could not read the thing. They should've asked my daughter to do it. She can read much better. Much, much better! She is prettier too! And I bought her designer clothes," Paige's mother said to another mother as they were leaving.

"They should've asked the boys to do it. They are born leaders," an unemployed father told another father. "I bought a brand-new suit, tie, and a pair of shoes for my son. Everything he is wearing is spanking brand-spanking-new. Besides, my son has the moral aptitude."

"You mean fortitude?" the other father asked with a smirk. "I thought you were going to file for bankruptcy. How could you afford to buy all of *that*?"

He chuckled. "That is the fun part. I put it all on my credit cards. I bought a shitload of stuff for myself and the wife. We won't have to pay a penny of it back."

All parents were outside at the end. They were complaining about something. Jennifer, her mother, and her uncle were the only ones who stayed behind, thanking the teacher and school principal.

Jennifer was wearing her new pink T-shirt. She showed the writing in front to her uncle and read it to him. Two lines in bold print read: **I'm the 2010 Graduate, Can I go to sleep now?** She did not know it, but Principal Williams' niece had received a similar T-shirt on her college graduation day; she had suggested it to Donna, and Miss Susan was the one who had located the vendor. Donna had purchased the T-shirt and decorating materials for the graduation event days in advance.

Jennifer also did not know that her grandparents were awaiting her at home. They had planned another small ceremony for her and decorated the house, and all the congratulatory signs were there too.

"We must go now," Donna told Susan and Principal Williams, and thanked them for the last time.

FADED SADDLE MOTORCYCLE SHOP

IT WAS 6:45 p.m. John, the floor manager, uttered the words that every salesman in the store had been waiting to hear for half an hour. "Bring them in!"

Within seconds the front double-door was wide open. Two pots, three feet in height and four feet in diameter, filled with potting soil, were located on each side of the door. Peter—the senior salesman at the Faded Saddle motorcycle dealership remembered when those pots contained lush green plants. That was a long time ago. The dealership was very different then. Now, the mammoth black pots were used as giant ashtrays. Customers and employees threw their cigarette butts there, in the pots, to get even with the management.

Peter remembered the previous general manager's famous words, "We're bound to have a miserable customer every now and then. We just can't make everyone happy." Nowadays, they had at least one angry customer for every happy one. Managers repeated the long-gone GM's statement behind closed doors—in meetings—but in response to the salesmen's complaint about unhappy customers they always said, "He just had a bad day. He is perfectly happy with his deal."

At the end of each day a salesman pushed the doors out from the center and secured them behind the round barren pots to keep the door in an open position as they rolled the used motorcycles inside the store. This was a Friday night. The staff and floor manager were planning to meet at a biker bar after work. They had invited Pete to join them on many such occasions. "I'm not much of a drinker, guys. I'll ruin it for all of you," he always responded with a benevolent smile. A few salesmen knew his profound reason for declining the invitations, he had no doubt. But some things were best kept secret, and his smile did just that.

One by one, they rolled the motorcycles inside. They were not allowed to start the engines, and each bike weighing between six to nine hundred pounds of sheer metal involved strenuous exercise to bring them in. The motorcycles could be anywhere from fifteen to fifty yards away. Every salesman was younger than Pete. Most of them were young enough to be his sons. Pursing his lips, and occasionally biting his lower lip, Pete looked like he was bench pressing as he struggled to roll them inside.

"Do you need help, Pete?"

"Would you like me to take that one?" other salesmen asked, and asked often.

"Thank you. I'm okay," Pete always responded.

"Mr. Peter, would you like to join us tonight," the new salesman said as they were logging out for the day. "It'll be fun," he added with a smile, as if he was inviting his own uncle.

Pete ran his fingers through his shaggy hair. Then he smiled and patted the young salesman on the shoulder, while the others watched. "It is so very kind of you to invite me, but my wife is waiting for me at home."

Pete was the only employee who could log out early and get away with it, but he was always the last one to log out, and tonight was no exception.

"Good night. See you tomorrow," Pete said in a fatherly voice, calling every salesman by name. They all replied cordially.

JOHN

John, the floor manager, had received his degree in geology from an Ivy League university. Among other things, he had played a great role in restoring New Orleans after Katrina. He drove a relatively new Mercedes-Benz and owned five Harley-Davidson motorcycles. "I'm not old enough to be retired," he told the salesmen. John took "the nonsense" from the upper management and tried to make sense of it. "Please do what I'm asking you to do and we all make money. If you have any issues, pull me aside and tell me privately. I can take the shit from you. I can be chewed up by Bob and eat a shit sandwich every day." John recognized his many nervous moments and considered them inescapable parts of his job. He worked hard to make everybody happy.

JACK

Jack was twenty-two years old. He had been the second runner-up, twice, for employee of the month. At the center of the parking lot, a parking spot was earmarked with a metal post. The plaque at the top of it read "Reserved for the Best." Employees voted once a month and the entire sales department—management as well as staff—had voted for him. His bushy beard and mustache distinguished him from the other salesmen. He had the demeanor of a Methodist pastor and talked softly with good diction. Many customers bought their bikes from him because they trusted him.

BRET

Bret was in his late forties. Years ago, he

studied economics in college. No one doubted that he would have received his PhD and could have been teaching economics today, had he continued. He was very smart, but he blamed his father for having to quit school. The youngest child of three, Bret was eighteen years old when his father announced that he was divorcing their mother. Among other things, Bret's father owned two nickel plants and an airport hangar. Bret worked harder than any other salesman and made a decent income. He never asked for money from his father. He had made a few mistakes in the past, but he admitted to each and every one of them, and had changed his ways. Once a motorcycle race driver, Bret was the most experienced and knowledgeable salesperson. But he was never snobbish about it.

MATT

Matt was twenty years old, with no college education. He had used his father's good credit to buy the cheapest motorcycle he could find. He had promised to keep this job until the last note on the bike had been paid, and he had no intention of reneging on his promise.

BIFF

An all-American boy, Biff was just as good on motorcycles as Bret. No one escaped his comely smile. Even the grouchiest and the grumpiest customers carried on a long and pleasant conversation with Biff. He knew a lot about the motorcycles. Between Biff and Bret, they could have presented their products as effectively as the engineers who built them. Many customers remained loyal to Biff because of the way he treated them.

AT THE BIKER BAR

"Why don't we sit over there?" Matt asked, pointing at a table on the other side of the room. Everyone recognized it immediately. The waitress—not the table—had seized his attention. They all looked at him and smiled.

"You do realize that this is not a nudie bar, Matt," John said, and led everyone in a different direction. "Kathy, do you have a table for me and my buddies?" he asked one of the waitresses.

Kathy counted everyone with her fingers and said, "Follow me, guys."

They sat at a round table. Kathy leaned on John and he wrapped his arm around her waist. She said, with a seductive smile, "Boys, you may have anything you see around here, but me."

"They already know. You're mine," John said.

"That'll be the day, grandpa," Kathy replied and pulled out her ordering pad without moving away from him.

"Drinks are on me. Give everybody a beer," John said and gave Kathy ten dollars. "Run me a tab. I'll put it on my credit card."

"Okay, big shot." Kathy looked at the money and put it inside her mini-apron pocket.

"You know we'll take care of you, Kathy," John said.

"You better!" Kathy looked around the table with a big smile.

"Wait a minute," interjected Biff. "We can't be drinking beer on empty stomachs. Let's have some chicken wings."

"I second that," said Bret. He knew Biff

was going to pay for the food. He passed him twenty dollars underneath the table and gave Kathy another ten. "This is for you, sweetheart. My buddy here will pay for the food."

"I like your buddies, John. They dig me."

Matt and Jack were the first ones to finish their beer. As Matt was drinking the last drops of his beer, he asked, "Does Pete drink?"

"You don't know much about the old man, do you? Pete used to be a bartender," said Bret.

"He is not that old, is he?" asked Jack.

"He is in his sixties, dude!" said Biff.

"Really? That's why it's so hard for him to roll the motorcycles," said Jack, "and he never lets me do it for him." There was a moment of silence.

"So what does he do for fun?" asked Matt.

"I don't think fun and Pete come in the same sentence," said Biff and there was a unanimous guffaw.

"Hey! Hey! Don't you guys pick on him enough at work?" said John and everybody became quiet.

"Dude, we really like him and respect him," said Bret.

It was after ten when they left the bar. Two of the guys left an hour after their arrival. As if they had planned it in advance, each drank only one beer and said he had promised to have dinner with his girlfriend.

John barely finished his second beer. Bret and Biff drank three beers each, but they stuffed themselves with chicken wings.

Matt drank more than everybody else, but he was adamant he would ride his bike home. "John, are you going to let him ride his bike?" Bret asked, whispering.

"You guys are leaving with me," John said, looking at Matt and Jack. "Leave your bike here tonight. It'll be safe here. Everyone knows me." He looked at Jack and said, "And no one will touch your jalopy."

Jack was still calm and collected in spite of all the alcohol he had consumed. "Why are you punishing me? I'm not drunk!" he protested.

"Work with me, dude! I can't fight him by myself," John replied, whispering.

Bret and Biff looked at Jack. "You better go with John too." There was a pause. "You ought to, dude." They were not telling him, but pleading with him, for the sake of Matt, and Jack recognized it quickly. He tapped Matt's shoulder and said, "We just drank more than we should've, buddy. John will drive us home."

"That was fun. John is a cool dude," Bret told Biff outside.

"We have a good team now. If only the management was not making it so difficult for us."

Bret nodded. "I'm glad that Jack did not put up a fight. There was nothing wrong with *him*."

"I know. It was Matt. He just bought that bike. And you have to know your limit, if you want to ride your bike home," Biff said.

"He would've gotten himself killed on his bike."

"That's for sure," Biff said, nodding.

Peter looked at his credit card bill and counted his money, soon after sitting in his car. *Why did I buy those designer shirts? I never wear them.* He had bought two shirts for himself while purchasing Christmas presents for his wife. That was months ago. He wanted to wear them when they went out for dinner together, but he could not afford to do it and she never asked him to take her out.

"One of these days," he whispered and started his car.

On the way to the store, Pete envisioned himself being at the bar with the guys. *I bet they are drooling over there, right now! Those chicks are something else. Damn it! If I did not have so much debt on my credit cards, I would've joined them. At least once!* He had used his credit cards to buy clothes for his wife, and groceries on a few occasions. He had also used them impulsively, more often than he would have admitted. He had very little debt on this department store credit card and felt victorious about paying it off completely.

At the parking lot in the mall, Pete counted his money once again. He entered the store, walking casually. He was a good window shopper, most of the time. *I bet she would love to have that bag. That skirt will look good on her.* He did not feel guilty if he bought something for his wife and she did not wear it.

Within minutes Pete was sheepishly standing in line, waiting his turn to pay his bill. The lady in front of him was dressed like a professional woman. Pete recognized that she was wearing fine material, but he could not identify the fabric. *Where did she buy her clothes? I wonder if my Sam would like something like that.* The lady's red glittery high heel shoes and white pearl necklace seized his attention. Sam *is as tall as this lady, without high heel shoes. She likes glittery shoes. I wonder if I could find her some here*. He had resisted the temptations and was standing in the line empty-handed. *Promises, promises. I never bought a pearl necklace for her.*

As he was daydreaming, something extraordinary happened to him. He met the most amazing family. An irresistible desire urged him to smile at them. And he did it effortlessly, as if they were long-lost dear relatives. The mother walked around the cashier counter and approached Pete. They shook hands. Pete was so overwhelmed with the mother's kind, unforseen and unexpected, gesture that he froze and did not say anything. He wanted to follow her and apologize for his inept behavior. But he knew it would've made it worse. He was also very embarrassed for not saying anything to her.

After paying off his credit card, Pete quickly left the store. Driving home he was asking the same nagging questions. He could not stop blaming himself for not talking with the mother.

"How was your day?" he asked his wife a minute after walking through the front door. As usual, she had not had her dinner. She was waiting for him.

"It was a good day," she replied. "I finished reading another novel. You know. The kind that you're not so crazy about." She read romance novels and detective series most of the time. "How was your day? Did you sell a motorcycle?"

Pete collapsed in the chair and faked a smile.

"How was your day?" she asked again. She could see stress on his face. That could not be from work. She was sure of it. Pete liked everyone, customers and employees, and they all liked him.

After a long pause, Pete sighed. "You *wouldn't believe* what happened to me today." He repeated everything that had happened at the department store, from the second the family walked through the door. "It was an incredible experience and *I blew it*! I could've said something. *Anything!*"

"You did a wonderful thing. You gave them a wonderful gift with your smile. You're just too harsh on yourself."

The more they talked, the more she realized that his insufficient response was the least of his concerns. "I wish I could write about this," Pete said as they were ending their conversation.

"Why don't you?" she responded.

Early on Sunday morning Pete was sitting in front of the computer. "Are you writing something?" Samantha asked.

"I'm trying to," Pete responded and did not elaborate.

"Let me see it when you finish."

"I will. If I can say what I am trying to say."

Hours later Pete showed Samantha a one-page computer printout. "This is what I wrote," he told her.

She put on her reading glasses and started reading it:

> Grace and generosity mean different things to different people. Having enough money to solve financial problems of fellow human beings is one way of accomplishing this. I personally don't know anyone who can—or—is willing to do it.
>
> Using a few clever sentences—and/or—suggesting a practical solution for a complicated personal problem is another way of achieving this. It is so unfortunate that God only gave us one Doctor Phil.
>
> I am an average person with very few resources. Still, occasionally coworkers tell me "You are a nice guy." I don't raise my voice at people and seem to be agreeable, at least most of the time.

But then again, being told you are a nice guy is not the same as genuine kindness and thoughtfulness. So, I have been accepting this kind comment quietly and humbly.

I don't remember the last time I wiped anyone's tears. Actually, I did not realize that I could do it, until now.

Less than twenty hours ago, as I was standing in a line at a store, three people walked inside together. They were a couple, walking with their daughter. The daughter seemed to be too reserved. I smiled at them. My smile was more pronounced because I thought the daughter was a special person. I wanted to welcome them to the store. It was just a simple and easy gesture, like shaking hands in the church. So I thought. But apparently my simple gesture meant more to them than I thought. A lot more!

The mother walked up to me. She had the smile of Mother Teresa. And if I was truly pious, I am sure I would have seen two angels on her shoulders.

"Thank you for your kind smile," she told me.

I was blind, occupied with my daily trivial life, and too embarrassingly naive to realize what was happening then. That couple probably has been swimming in their own ocean of tears, because we are incapable of smiling at all children, all the time.

I wiped their tears without realizing it. Or so it seemed to me.

It is a sad world indeed!

I am not sure if I should be proud of myself for wiping their tears, or, if I should be ashamed of myself for not realizing that I was reaching out and touching this family.

WHO WAS "BO BO"?

IN HER FIFTIES, she was walking with her son inside the grocery store. She was short and scrawny, as he was tall and bulky. As if life had taken its toll on her, she was slouching and walking at a slow pace. Her iron gray hair, with a slight natural curl, was combed back with care and diligence. Stubbornly, she had kept her thick hair, in spite of her age. It covered her nape majestically. Her dark gray, long-sleeved blouse matched her loose, long pants—only in color; her dull black flat shoes were as ageless as the rest of her clothes; and she wore no costume jewelry.

She held up a can of food. "Bo Bo, do you like this one?" she asked in a motherly voice.

Six and a half feet tall, Bo Bo was standing unnervingly close to his mother. He bent his huge upper torso above her head and said, "I don't want it! Put it back!"

What kind of a name is Bo Bo? I asked myself. I could not figure out if Bo Bo was disappointed, angry, or both. He certainly displayed a childlike tantrum.

Bo Bo did not say anything else and walked to the other end of the aisle—with conspicuous disrespect. He examined several cans of tuna, as well as other items on the shelf—one by one. "They are not *that expensive,*" he said several times, and kept raising his voice. She continued looking at the more essential items on their list of groceries and tried her best to ignore him.

He must be thirty years old, if not older! In an instant, I could not help myself, but to compare Bo Bo with Alex.

Alex was a senior in high school when his mother received full custody of him. Susan,

Alex's mother, talked about her son with enthused motherly fever. "I'm so glad!" "My son has finally moved away from his abusive father." "He is staying with me now!" "I will raise him properly." "I will love him and care for him, as he deserves to be loved and cared for."

Everybody was so happy to see the mother and son's reunion, but this did not last for long.

"My teachers are stupid! I don't want to go to school anymore!" Alex told Susan.

"That's okay, dear," Susan responded. "You don't want to go to school. You don't have to. You don't have to do anything you don't want to."

Friends and relatives were shocked by the news.

"Just like that?" everyone asked Susan. "He said 'My teachers are stupid and I don't want to go to school,' and that was your *response? And you are okay with it?"*

"I went to college! I went to graduate school! It did not do me much good! Why should I make my dear son go to school if he doesn't want to?" Susan told everyone.

No one could believe what they were hearing.

Alex was an adolescent, and no one was completely shocked to hear what he had said about his teachers. After all, many parents had heard similar comments from their children. But Susan was a seasoned social worker, an intelligent and extremely educated woman. We could condone Alex's unyielding behavior due to his age, but Susan's foolish and reckless accommodation was completely insane, we thought.

I grabbed what I needed quickly and moved to the next aisle. So did the mother and son. Once again I was a captive audience. Their interaction became more bizarre and schizophrenic by the second. Bo Bo was silent and uncommunicative until he noticed something on the shelf. Then he demanded it.

"I want it!" he said loudly and disrespectfully—every time.

"But, dear," she said sheepishly.

"I said, I want it!" He raised his voice every time.

I could not believe what I was hearing. *What is this? How could this be? She is the mother. Why does she let her son talk to her in this manner? In this tone of voice!* I left the store as fast as I could.

Driving home, I could not stop thinking about Bo Bo. I was really feeling sorry for his mother. I wanted to laugh and cry at the same time, and I probably would have, had I not been driving. I wanted to believe Bo Bo's behavior, or rather what I had witnessed, was an aberration, an anomaly, a bad dream. Instead, I remembered a personal experience with another acquaintance, a long time ago.

At the time, I was doing support groups for people who had been through personal crises. It was an extension of my job as a patient advocate. A hardworking mother, a single parent, once approached me at the end of our group session. She asked me to talk to her daughter.

"My daughter is very smart. She is very good with computers," she told me.

"So, what seems to be the problem?" I asked.

She sighed. "She thinks she has schizophrenia."

"Really! Who told her that?" I asked, expecting to hear a professional diagnosis, a doctor's opinion.

She lowered her head and sighed again. "Nobody. I have brought her to see several psychiatrists, and they all think there's nothing wrong with her."

"So, why can't she get a job and stay out of your hair?" I asked as if it was a no-brainer.

"That's why I want you to talk to her. She won't." The mother was pleading, but I really did not want to get involved. I was hired to help adults. I had no medical training and my college degree was in political science. I was a good listener, a trustworthy person, and somewhat persuasive. That was why I was effective at my job. The only other training was reading extensively about the symptoms of different forms of mental disorders. I had no psychiatric training.

"I'd like to help you, but I'm not sure if I'm the right person," I said.

"Please! I don't have any other recourse.

I don't know anyone else. You must help me. I'm begging you! Just talk to her!" She showed me her pictures, from toddler to teen. "I think she needs a father figure," she said and told me how much she was missing her father.

I finally agreed to see the daughter.

I had mentally prepared myself to see a young woman with several tattoos on her neck, arms, and legs. She had no tattoos, at least none visible. She did not have a ring in her tongue, or her nose. She wore a small set of earrings, and exhibited good taste and simple style. Her clothes were just as humble and unassuming. Had I not known better, I would have presumed she was a teacher, or a librarian.

"This is my daughter, Peaches," her mother said.

Peaches? Really? Does she have a name? I could have appreciated it if she wanted to call her Peaches in the privacy of their home. I could also have understood if she wanted me to call her Peaches after we got to know each other, but using such a nickname for introductory purposes seemed unusual, if not bizarre.

I felt like asking the mother. Does she have a name, like Susan, or Penny?

Peaches was just as smart as her mother claimed. She talked about her high school days enthusiastically and showed me several pictures, taken with her classmates.

"Have you been in touch with them?" I asked.

She shrugged. "They go to college. I don't see them anymore. Some even have jobs," she said.

"Don't you want to go to college? Don't you want to have a job?"

"No. I don't care for college. I don't want to work."

"Don't you want to see your former classmates?"

"I had a date with one of them, a cute guy. But he is a geek now. You know! A college boy! He did not call me back. I think he freaked out when I told him that I don't want to work."

"Why not? Why don't you want to have a job?" I asked, puzzled.

She shrugged and looked at me as if I was

the crazy one. "Why should I? My mother pays all my bills. I have all her credit cards." She pulled out two credit cards. "You see. These credit cards are in my name."

"How did you manage to get yourself a credit card?" I asked. "You don't have a job!"

She smiled. "It's really Mom's. I used her account, but it has my name and she pays them. No worries. It's legit."

I couldn't figure her out. *Is she mimicking us? Is she being sarcastic? Is that her idea of a joke?* I was hard-pressed to come up with a word and did not say anything. I was very familiar with the concept of enabling a person with bad behavior. I left, vowing not to visit them ever again. A week later her mother contacted me and told me her daughter had a job offer. "A good one," she assured me.

"How do you know?"

"It's a computer job. She does not even have to leave home, to go to work. She'll do what she is already doing with her computer. She'll do what she loves to do. And she'll get paid for it."

The person who had offered her daughter

the job knew the mother. He was sure that the daughter would accept the job offer.

The mother invited me to their house. She pleaded with me to share her joy and pulled the "father figure" card once again.

I agreed, against my better judgment. We met outside her work place and drove to her house.

We were both mentally exhausted, and the mother was even more stressed out than I was.

"Why do you have to be so damn noisy, Mother? You woke me up. You should know better. I was up all night playing games on my computer," Peaches exclaimed as soon as we walked inside.

"I know, dear. I could not sleep last night. Your bedroom is next to mine and I kept hearing those strange noises from your computer." The mother was acting as if *she* owed her daughter an apology.

"Don't you understand? Are you stupid? That's the only joy I have in life, other than watching TV. You won't take me out for dinner every night. What do you expect?"

After hearing several "Yes dears," Peaches told her mother about the news. "I checked my emails today. Some idiot offered me a job. An Internet job. 'You may work at home and get paid well,' he wrote. Can you believe it?"

"How did you respond, dear," the mother asked timidly.

"Do you really have to ask? Of course I declined the offer. I told him why do I need a job? My mother pays all the bills." She shrugged. "Why do I need to work?"

"But, dear, you won't go to college. I offered to drive you to school___"

"I hate college! How many times do I have to tell you? I have schizophrenia!"

"But, dear, the psychiatrist told me you were fine."

"What does that stupid doctor know? He is not in my head! You should've found me a good psychiatrist, one who agrees with me."

"But, dear, we have seen other psychiatrists. They all have said the same thing." She sighed.

"We've been through this, Mother! I don't want to talk about it!"

The daughter walked back to her room and slammed the door behind her. The mother just looked at me helplessly.

How could it be? What's wrong with these people? I asked myself, walking in the house.

"You look preoccupied. What happened at the grocery store?" my wife asked me.

Biting my lower lip, I shook my head and did not say anything.

"What happened at the grocery store?" she asked again.

"You wouldn't believe it if I told you. I saw something ridiculous. *Completely insane!*"

We talked about Bo Bo and his mother. Her reaction was a mixture of disbelief and denial—so I thought. She listened to me patiently, smiled, and said something profound—yet so simple. "You do know that there is a bit of Bo Bo in every one of us."

Suddenly, I couldn't think of anything to say. *Oh, my God!* What she said was so truthful—and so scary.

MADARJOON

This story is dedicated to my late grandmother.

WE DIDN'T KNOW her real name or her age. We just called her *Madar Joon,* an Iranian term of endearment meaning grandmother. Her room was on the second floor of our house. As a child, in her absence, my cousin and I used to go to her room to chase each other around her *corsey*—a square wooden box covered with a huge square blanket. At the bottom of the box is a metal tray filled with hot charcoal. It is very popular in Iran, and on cold winter days family members sit around the corsey and cover their bodies with the blanket. We both knew running around her room was unacceptable behavior. But that was our favorite thing. We were her grandsons at a tender age, and Madar Joon never complained.

I also remember when she had a bedding arrangement for my baby sister in her room. It was the Iranian equivalent of a hammock designed for babies, a cushiony pouch hung by two long ropes from the opposite walls. It was very safe and comfortable and my sister loved it more than anything else. Madar Joon had attached a rope to the center of the pouch. She gently pulled the pouch and swung it as my sister fell asleep.

Those were the sweet memories of my grandmother before I entered grammar school. Now, decades after her passing, I have learned an incredible story about her. I look back at those precious moments and wonder about this most extraordinary woman, my dearest Madar Joon.

CHAPTER ONE

Recently widowed, Battool lived with her

two sons, who were less than ten years apart. Ali was twelve years old. Rezza, her younger son, was still playful and childishly manipulative. Young and ill-equipped to deal with their father's death, the two boys took two different routes to cope with their tragic loss.

The older son gave up his private art lessons and quit school.

"Ali, you're very talented. You mustn't quit. You must follow your heart, pursue your passion, and become an artist," Ali's art teacher, a good friend of his late father, pleaded with him. Ali did not argue with his teacher; nor did he take his advice. He drew patterns for expensive Persian rugs and sold them to a businessman who had hired weavers to produce them. His income was not as much as his father's was, but it was enough to support the family's basic needs.

The younger son also quit school. He wanted to remain a child for as long as he could. That was his way of protesting their father's early demise. At times, Rezza slammed the door repeatedly, demanding money. Ali never gave in, nor did he become abusive toward his younger brother. He just ignored his annoying behavior.

"Rezza, your brother works very hard to support us. You mustn't treat him this way," Battool pleaded in a motherly voice.

As most women in her situation did, Battool weaved rugs. She could not do it as efficiently as a professional weaver, and her monetary contribution was miniscule. But that was the best she could do to help out financially.

The only valuable thing she owned was a ring with a precious stone. "I would like you to sell my ring for me. I want to give the money to Ali," she told her older brother every time he visited them.

Her brother looked at her, then looked at the ring every time, and said, "This is the only thing you own. I can't sell it for you. You must keep it! This ring is just as precious as you are."

"But I must help Ali!"

"Ali is strong and determined. He's making enough money. You must keep your ring."

A year after their father's death, Rezza was still not showing any interest in going back to school.

"Leave me alone! You're my brother. You're not my father!" he told Ali.

"I'm your older brother and I'm supporting you and our mother. I was in school when our father was alive. I'm doing this now to support us. I'm working hard so you can go back to school."

"Just leave me alone! I don't want to go back to school."

"Mother, why don't you make Rezza go back to school?" Ali asked Battool.

"Ali joon, he is still a child. He's not as mature as you are. He is still missing his father."

"But you are our mother. You must put your foot down. He'll have to listen to you. He needs to go back to school."

Battool always made a plate of food for Ali first. "You mustn't work so hard. Maybe you should be attending school a couple of days a week," she told Ali every now and then.

"Mother, I'm taking care of the family. I have to work. You should be worrying about Rezza."

Battool didn't want to see Ali work so hard. *He's not much older than Rezza.* She looked at Ali and saw a boy who was forced to act like an adult. It brought pain to her heart and tears to her eyes. But she couldn't let Ali feel her pain or see her tears. She looked at Rezza and saw a disgruntled child who was refusing to recognize a cruel world and abide by its rules. *What will happen to him? He's not as talented as Ali. Ali can read and write. He speaks like an educated man. Rezza does not!* Although not mentioning it to Ali, she worried about Rezza, more than Ali did.

AND THE STORY CONTINUES.

A PEEK THROUGH A BROKEN NEST

CHUCK

In his late forties, Chuck had walked through many peaks and valleys. A serene and quiet life he never had. He had worked hard for a few personal accomplishments over the years. Well educated, once he was considered a promising graduate student. Many of his peers—with far less potential—had reached their dreams years earlier. They had a career and a family, but Chuck was never so lucky. He started becoming bitter and angry soon after leaving graduate school. After his parents passed on, he had to fight an adversary more vicious than any in the past. He was diagnosed with chronic depression. That was years ago. Since, Chuck had accepted his fate and concluded that anger and bitterness would only make him cold and unpleasant. That was not who Chuck was.

Chuck was not sure why he was fascinated—if indeed he was—with casinos. His first encounter was years earlier. After applying for a job at a casino in New Orleans, he met one of his former college classmates inside. His friend was sitting at a blackjack table. "It's so good to see you, Chuck," Bill told him. "I sold my share of the business to my partner. My wife is from New Orleans and she wanted to move back here." Bill talked about his wife and their newborn son. He talked about his career opportunities. Chuck listened and nodded occasionally. Bill lost two-hundred dollars. *I wonder how it feels to be able to afford to lose that kind of money,* Chuck thought as they were leaving.

AMANDA

"Are you reading your diary again?" Biff

screamed at Amanda, his girlfriend. She was in their bedroom; he was in their bathroom—doing his ritual. Looking at his face in the mirror, Biff mimicked an expression that had been rehearsed many times. In his mind, it had become uniquely his. Combing his hair and his goatee, he repeated it with tremendous joy, "Oh yeah! You've got it, Biff." He had mastered the art of narcissism.

"I'm ready. Where are we going?" Amanda replied.

"You damn well know where we're going tonight!"

"Not the casino again. You'll lose all your money. Have you paid the rent?"

"Not to worry. The rent is paid. We won't lose our palace. Put your best clothes on. I'm going to win a lot of money tonight."

"You always say that!"

"I mean it this time. I'm going to win *big* tonight. I'll buy you something nice tomorrow."

Biff did not know what was in Amanda's diary, nor did he know how current it was. She had only read a few lines of it to him. That was so long ago, at the beginning of their relationship. He was sweet and romantic then. She thought Biff was her prince charming and liked his goatee. That was why she had shared an important part of herself with him.

"Put that damn diary aside before I come over there and take it from you. I'll throw it away. Something I should've done a long time ago."

Biff always threatened to take her diary and destroy it. Amanda believed him and hid it. But that was just Biff's way of tormenting her. He was convinced that there were only rosy memories of her past in that diary. He wanted Amanda to read it to herself and cry over it. That was a source of pleasure for Biff and he had no intention of taking the diary away from her.

Intrigued, as if this was the first time for him, Chuck gingerly entered the casino. Countless tiny little stars grabbed his attention immediately. Red, blue, yellow, white, and incredibly bright, they turned on and off in an oval pattern above the slot machines. There was the sound of laughter, cursing, screaming, and of course the music, but none was as loud and powerful as the winning sounds generated by the slot machines. Empty cushiony stools were demanding occupants.

Chuck did what he had been doing. He walked in the middle and across the room, ignoring everything that interested everybody else. There were blackjack tables, two giant roulette tables, two craps tables, and a three-card poker table on the right side. Most of the slot machines were on the left side. The main bar was across the room, and the coffee station—Chuck's favorite spot—was next to it.

Away from the regulars and occasional visitors, Chuck was an island by himself, drinking coffee and observing. That was until now. Tonight, Chuck was going to share his ground with another islander.

Looking at her face from an angle, he felt an immediate attraction and thought about starting a conversation with her. As he reached for cream and sugar, his arm was very close, almost touching her face.

"Am I being rude?" he asked sheepishly.

"Do you want to be rude to me?" Amanda responded. She was looking at him directly, with a smile that invites a lover for more intimacy. As she continued, her smile became more appealing. "You're not being rude at all!"

She must have been a beautiful woman, once. She cannot be that old! Why has she withered so much? Chuck thought.

Sipping their coffee, Amanda and Chuck walked a few yards away from the coffee machine. Away from the players—together—they were in their own little place.

"Where are you from? Are you originally from Baton Rouge?" Chuck asked.

"I can't hear you from this ear," Amanda said, pointing to her right ear. "I was kicked in my face by someone who is supposed to protect me."

Chuck disguised his shock with a fake smile and did not say anything. There was nothing more horrific that Amanda could have said to him. Her gentle tone could not hide her pain; nor could it diminish the brutality of this act, at least not in Chuck's mind.

Such innocence. Such a cruel world, Chuck thought. After a pause Amanda talked again. Her voice became gentler and more penetrating. They were looking at the other players at the casino, but neither one of them wanted to depart. There was a strong and invisible connection between them; they could not simply walk away from each other.

"I must go sit with my friend," Amanda finally said and pointed toward a distant slot machine. "You probably have to do the same."

Chuck resisted an incredibly strong urge and did not ask her to stay. It was clear to him that she was talking about her boyfriend, or her husband. He only mumbled, "Are you sure?" When she left, he stayed behind and sipped his coffee, but the inferno was not quieting down. *What happened to her? Where is she?* He was looking in different directions. *There she is! That must be her boyfriend.*

Amanda was sitting next to her boyfriend Biff, on the other side of the casino. They were sitting in front of a slot machine. He kept pulling the handlebar and cursing. She was subdued and disengaged.

Why? Chuck asked himself.

Within minutes, Biff moved away from the slot machine and sat at a blackjack table. Amanda did not move. Earshot distance from Biff, she remained seated on a stool.

"Come here! Stand next to me!" Biff demanded harshly.

She ignored his demand and remained seated.

"Come here! Stand next to your man!" Biff demanded, more brutally this time.

She moved to the blackjack table, stood next to him. "Can we leave? Please!" she whispered in his ear.

"No! I have to make some money! I have to win my money back. Be quiet!" Biff said. He was so loud that everyone—even people at the other tables—could hear him.

Looking at them from a distance, Chuck could understand the body language, as if he was hearing them. He noticed an empty seat at the blackjack table and thought *I should go there and sit next to them.* Then he hesitated momentarily.

"Did you want to play? There's an empty

spot there," one of the players told Chuck, as soon as he walked to the table.

"I'm thinking about it," Chuck replied nonchalantly.

"Give your girlfriend some chips. Make her sit down and play. We don't want that man here!" another player, an older man, a regular, told Biff.

Biff gave Amanda two red chips. "Sit down and play," he told her. His voice was not harsh this time.

"I don't want to play," Amanda said timidly.

"You don't have to play. Just sit down."

Amanda took the chips, sat down, and whispered to Biff, "Can we go home? Please!"

"No! Just be quiet! We'll go home when I'm ready!" Biff sounded harsh and brutal again.

"Ma'am, you have to play or give up your seat. I believe the gentleman behind you wants to play," the floor supervisor stated.

"Don't you move, sweetheart. You're fine where you are," the older man told Amanda and turned toward the supervisor. "That man is new to the game. He does not know how to play! He'll ruin it for all of us!" He was referring to Chuck.

"I'm sorry, but you have to stand up and let the man behind you play" said the supervisor more firmly. He was looking at Amanda and ignoring the older man.

"I have to stand up. They'll make us leave if I don't," Amanda told Biff in a timid voice.

"You don't have to get up. I'm not sure if I want to play," Chuck said bashfully.

"That's okay. I'm not playing," Amanda responded.

Hesitantly, Chuck put a ten-dollar bill on the table. "Please sit down. I'll play standing up," he told Amanda.

"Are you sure?" Amanda waited for Chuck's approval before sitting down.

"I'm positive! Please sit down. I'm quite comfortable standing up."

"He's a piece of work. He only has ten dollars and wants to ruin it for all of us." The older man looked at Chuck with contempt.

"Damn it! I lost again!" Biff said, and hit the table hard with his fist.

He'll take it out on me tonight. I can't lose

my hearing completely. Amanda leaned on Biff romantically and pleaded with him. "Let's leave now, honey. You still have some money. Let's leave now. Please!"

Biff pushed her away. "No! I know what I'm doing! I have to win my money back!"

Within ten minutes Chuck had lost his money. He stood behind the players, thinking about Amanda and Biff. *What will happen to her? Will he beat her up again?*

None of the players seemed to care about Amanda. They only cared about winning their money back. They high-fived Biff every time the dealer had more than twenty-one and paid them; they ignored Biff's behavior every time he became obnoxious and irritable.

Chuck looked inside his wallet. He had money, but did not want to gamble anymore. *I wonder if the jerk would leave with her should I cover his loss.* He was fighting the temptation to bet his last ten dollars, just to be around for a few more minutes.

Amanda was too scared to look at Chuck. *Just hang around. You don't have to play,* she thought.

"Go find me a cocktail waitress. I need a beer!" Biff ordered Amanda.

"I need one too, sweetheart," the older man said. "Find us a cocktail waitress. We all need a drink."

Chuck thought about following Amanda, but she gave him a look that discouraged him. Slowly and hesitantly, Chuck walked toward the exit door. As he was leaving, he turned around and looked at Amanda. *I will be back again. I will see you again.*

She was walking around aimlessly, looking for a cocktail waitress.

Amanda looked at Chuck as he stepped out of the casino. His back was toward her and he could not see her. *I can't wait to write about us in my diary. I will see you again,* she thought.

The next morning, after Biff left for work, Amanda pulled out her diary from its secret spot and start writing.

Something amazing happened to me last night.

She thought for a moment and continued writing.

"What did you do last night?" a friend asked Chuck.

"Something I should've never done. Something I'll never do again," Chuck replied. He had promised himself never to go back to the casino.

WHO WAS GRJ?

AS TALL AND muscular as he was, it was the way he approached the altar that impressed me. He walked with the humility of a saint and the confidence of a king.

He walked up to the altar and stepped behind the lectern. With no hesitation he introduced himself as the "best friend" of the deceased. "I am climbing the mountain, Jack! I am climbing the mountain that you have climbed, Jack!" He talked about their youth, when they felt invincible. "Do you remember those days, Jack? Do you remember our football days in high school? You taught me how to play football. I wanted to be a star! A star just like you, Jack!"

Who is Jack? I asked myself. He must have said "Jack" a dozen times before I realized that he was talking about the deceased. By then, I had also concluded that this man was successful, very successful professionally, and he must have stood behind many lecterns, many times.

Does he know that he had been using crack!? I asked myself.

"Why do I always make Cs and Ds? Why can't I make As and Bs, like you do?' I used to ask Jack. He always had the same answer. 'Our teachers would know that I am doing your homework if we made the same grades.'"

Really? Is he talking about the same guy? The deceased had been clean for two years before passing. Still, I could not believe that this man was genuinely acknowledging him this way. *As a mentor?*

"I honestly don't know how many times Jack bailed me out. 'This is the last time that I'm helping you with your homework,' Jack told me many times, but we both knew I could've never made it without his help. He said the same thing when we went to college. 'Now we're in college. You'll be on your own.'" He paused to compose himself. His voice was cracking and I could see the pain on his face. "But that did not stop me from asking him to write my papers..."

GRJ was the man who I had developed a tremendous respect for in the last two years of his life, as he had defeated the demon of chemical dependency. On the day of the funeral I sat in front of the church as one of the pallbearers. This was truly an honor for me. Although I am a close friend of the family, I had not met this particular mourner before the funeral, nor have I met him since. But I cannot stop asking myself what "Jack" meant to him. I have tried many times, since, to imagine the impact of the word "Jack" on this man's mind, heart, and soul, each and every time he uttered it in the church on that particular day.

CPSIA information can be obtained
at www.ICGtesting.com
Printed in the USA
BVHW070808150419
545531BV00001B/264/P
9 781977 203816